What The Amish Heart Wants

Stephanie Swift

Published by Trellis Publishing, 2021.

WHAT THE AMISH HEART WANTS

First edition. July 5, 2021.

ISBN: 979-8224232000

Written by Stephanie Swift.

WHAT THE AMISH HEART WANTS

STEPHANIE SWIFT

WHAT THE AMISH HEART WANTS

STEPHANIE SWIFT

Gloria Sommer gazed out her kitchen window and smiled as she watched her fiancé, Lloyd Smith, slowly make his way from the barn to her house. His clothes were dirty and disheveled, and as he took of his hat and wiped his brow with the back of his shirt sleeve, she noticed he also had some dark smudges on his cheeks. She went to the refrigerator and retrieved a pitcher of fresh lemonade just as he walked through the side door and into the room.

"I take it the horses wouldn't go willingly into the barn," she said, motioning to his rugged attire.

Lloyd looked down at his clothing and chuckled. "*Yah*. A couple of them weren't too happy about having their hooves shoed either."

He turned over his left arm, and Gloria gasped when she saw a large blood stain on his sleeve. He unbuttoned it at the wrist and pulled it up to reveal a long gash on his arm.

"Oh no! I'm so sorry, Lloyd. Was it Bella again?"

She grabbed a dish cloth from one of the kitchen drawers and wet it in the sink before placing it against the wound. The cut didn't appear deep enough to require stitches, but it would probably leave a nasty scar.

"I've tried charming her into liking me, but it hasn't worked. That horse is determined to make my life miserable."

He laughed as he said it, but Gloria knew he was close to his wit's end with Bella. The mare was one of the best horses her father owned for plowing, but her bedside manner left a lot to be desired.

"Maybe she's just jealous because you pay more attention to me than her," Gloria joked.

While Lloyd took a seat at the kitchen table, she went to an overhead cabinet and gathered a box of bandages and an herbal ointment handcrafted from a family recipe that had been passed down through several generations.

"Well, I hate to break her heart, but that's never going to change," he replied.

As Gloria sat across from him and doctored his injury, a mischievous smile danced across his handsome face, which made her blush. Even with his rumpled clothing, dirt-streaked face, and messy hair, he was still the most handsome man she'd ever met. He was also a hard worker, which was evident in his callused hands and the taut muscles that strained his shirt, which she tried her best not to stare at too long or too often.

"Have you decided on a Thanksgiving or Christmas wedding?" she asked.

Talking about their upcoming nuptials was the best way she could think of to occupy her mind and keep it from drifting to the warmth of his skin beneath her fingers. As she smoothed the ointment over the cut, she could almost hear her parents and the Bishop in her ear, reprimanding her for having such "wicked thoughts".

"I know this is our wedding, Gloria, but I also know it's the day you've been dreaming about since you were a little girl. I want you to make that decision. It doesn't matter to me when or where we get married as long as I get to spend the rest of my life with you."

His sweet sentiment brought the heat to her cheeks again, and she turned her attention back to her task so he wouldn't notice.

"Then I vote for Thanksgiving. It's only two months away, and I say the sooner the better."

He nodded and smiled. "That sounds like the perfect plan to me."

When Gloria finished dressing Lloyd's wound, she busied herself pouring two glasses of lemonade while he went to the bathroom to wash his face and hands. It was nearing four o'clock in the afternoon, and he would be leaving for his own house soon – a fact that always wilted her spirits. She looked forward to the day she wouldn't have to say "goodbye" to him after he finished his work.

A loud noise outside caught Gloria's attention and stopped her in her tracks. It sounded like a vehicle coming down the main road, which was highly unusual, since the English people from Lancaster rarely visited their small Amish community just outside the city limits. The last time she could recall seeing a vehicle pass by her house was three years prior when a taxi picked up her next-door neighbors, the Graber's, who had to board an emergency flight to Ohio to visit a sick relative.

Lloyd entered the room, and Gloria held a finger to her lips to keep him silent so she could listen. "Do you hear that?" she whispered.

He stopped and listened too, and seconds later a flash of light illuminated the kitchen as a car pulled into her driveway and startled them both. Gloria walked quickly to the window. "It's Sheriff Hawkins."

With Lloyd following closely on her heels, she walked outside to greet him, and Gloria could tell right away that something wasn't right. She'd known the sheriff since childhood, and he was always friendly and cooperative with the Amish people. He'd helped them many times when they were in dire straits, and she considered him a friend among the few English people she knew.

As he approached them, Gloria noticed worry lines crinkling his forehead, and the nervous way he chewed on his lower lip didn't put her at ease either. Her heart thumped erratically as she hurried her steps to reach him.

"*Goedemiddag*, Sheriff Hawkins! What brings you here? I trust you're doing well?"

The elderly man, who was seldom seen without a smile, had never appeared more serious, and when he took off his hat and began twirling it around and around his hand, Gloria knew without a doubt that something was terribly wrong.

"Good afternoon, Miss Gloria. I wish I was here under different circumstances, but I'm afraid I have some bad news. Your mother collapsed at the market a little while ago, and she was transported to the hospital by ambulance. It appears she may have had a stroke."

Gloria grabbed Lloyd's forearm to try and remain steady on her feet. It felt as if the wind had been thrust from her lungs, making it hard to breathe.

"I apologize for being so blunt, but we need to get you to the hospital right away. Your father and sister rode in the ambulance with her, and they'll meet us there."

She wanted to speak, but it was if she'd suddenly lost the ability to form words, and all she could do was nod. She felt physically ill, and for a moment she worried she might be sick in the sheriff's presence. Gloria inhaled deeply to try and calm her nerves.

"I'll get your things," Lloyd said. "I'm going with you."

He helped her to the sheriff's car and opened the back door so she could slide inside. As she sat on the back seat, with her heart pounding wildly in her chest, she watched as Lloyd talked to the sheriff. Their words were muted over the sound of the car engine running, but the concerned look on her fiancé's face was unmistakable.

When Lloyd left to go back inside the house to retrieve her clutch and house keys, Sheriff Hawkins returned to the driver's seat. The air in the small space was stifling and she felt very uncomfortable, having never ridden in an English vehicle before.

"Sheriff Hawkins, I know you will tell me the truth. Do you believe my mother will be alright?"

He didn't answer her right away, which only increased her anxiety. He glimpsed at her through the rear-view mirror and flashed her a half-hearted smile. "Miss Gloria, I honestly don't know. She was unresponsive when the EMT's arrived on the scene. I wish I could tell you she'll be just fine, but I'm not going to fill you with false hope because that wouldn't be right."

Gloria laced her hands together on top of her lap and nodded. She understood what he meant, and she appreciated his honesty, but it didn't relieve the sense of dread that settled in her bones and wouldn't let go.

Lloyd returned to the vehicle and climbed into the back seat with her, and soon they were veering away from her home and racing toward Lancaster. Sheriff Hawkins turned on what Lloyd called his emergency flashers, and as they flew past the trees along the empty dirt road, she could see the bright red lights dancing off the leaves.

She wanted to cry, and if she hadn't been in the men's presence, she would have let the tears fall where they may. Instead, she held on to Lloyd's hand and squeezed. He in turn massaged the back of her hand, and the soothing effect was a welcome balm she desperately needed.

"Pray with me," she pleaded. Her voice cracked, and she swallowed hard to keep from falling apart.

Lloyd nodded, and as they both bowed their heads and closed their eyes, he prayed out loud, asking the Lord for her mother's complete healing and for His mercy and grace that surpassed all understanding. It was a heartfelt request, and not only did it bring her a greater sense of peace, but it also reminded her how fortunate she was to have such a loving, God-fearing man as her soon-to-be husband.

Although it took just a few minutes to reach the hospital, it seemed to take much longer. As Sheriff Hawkins came to a stop outside the emergency room entrance, the three of them wasted no time in exiting the vehicle and hurrying inside. The lights in the massive building were bright and blinding and something Gloria wasn't used to, and she squinted as she searched through the crowd in the waiting room for a familiar face.

"Gloria!"

She turned to see who was calling her name when she was suddenly wrapped in little arms as her younger sister, Amy, grabbed her and held on tight. She was sobbing and trembling terribly, and Gloria kissed the top of her head and hugged her close to her body.

"It's okay, Amy," she soothed. "Everything is going to be alright."

Her father appeared by her side, and the look on his face sent a chill through Gloria's body. His face was pale and his eyes were bloodshot, possibly from crying. She couldn't be certain though. In nineteen years, the only time she'd witnessed him cry was when his parents passed away.

"Lloyd, why don't you take Amy to get something to drink? There's a water fountain just around the corner there."

He pointed to a nearby corridor, and when Lloyd managed to pry Amy away from Gloria, he gave her an anxious look before putting his arm across Amy's shoulders and leading her away. Her father motioned her and Sheriff Hawkins toward some empty seats in the corner of the room, and Gloria's feet felt as if they were made of lead as she slowly walked toward them. Several horrible scenarios flashed through her mind at once, and by the time she sat down, her stomach had twisted into one giant knot.

"I talked to one of the nurses a few minutes ago, and they're still trying to get Ruth stabilized. They're doing something called a CT scan, which will take pictures of her brain, but as of right now it appears she suffered a stroke. We won't know the extent of it until the results come back, but the nurse said someone will come talk to us as soon as they can get her vitals regulated."

He gave her arm an affectionate squeeze, but Gloria was so numb she barely felt it. In the space of just a few minutes, her whole life had been turned upside down. If her mother didn't pull through this, she would be the only relative left in their community to care for her father and Amy, and her marriage would have to be postponed – possibly indefinitely. It was a humbling thought that weighed heavy on her heart.

She wanted to talk, but she was so overcome with emotion, she didn't know if she would be able to utter a word without breaking down in tears. Lloyd and Amy returned a few minutes later, and as the others talked amongst themselves, Gloria stared blankly ahead, lost in her own thoughts and wishing she could snap her fingers and change their circumstances.

It wasn't long before the double doors to the ER opened and a nurse appeared. She scoured the room, and when her gaze fell on Gloria's father, she proceeded in their direction. He stood immediately, but Gloria's knees were wobbly, and it took her a few seconds before she trusted her legs to keep her upright.

After introductions were made, the nurse ushered them through the double doors to the emergency room, where they were met by a young male doctor who couldn't have been more than thirty years old.

"Dr. Wallace, this is Ruth Beller's husband, William, and their daughters, Gloria and Amy," the nurse explained.

The doctor acknowledged them with a nod of his head before he stuffed his hands inside his coat pockets and looked down at the floor. Gloria braced for the worst.

"Mr. Beller, we were able to get your wife's blood pressure and other vitals stable, and we performed a CT scan, which confirmed she had an ischemic stroke. She is experiencing some paralysis and weakness on the left side of her body. It may take a few weeks for her to completely return to her normal, everyday activities, but I believe with the right medicine and physical therapy she should be just fine."

For the first time in what felt like an eternity, Gloria was able to breathe properly. Her eyes swelled with tears as the anxiety and fear from the past two hours started to diminish. Amy rocked back and forth on her heels and clapped her hands excitedly.

"I realize that because of your faith and customs, you don't believe in conventional medicine, and I respect that, but this was a medical emergency. If your wife hadn't received immediate treatment, her odds of surviving this type of stroke would have been very slim."

Her father nodded. "I understand...and thank you. When can we see her?"

The doctor glanced at his watch. "She's still heavily sedated, so it will be at least a couple of hours before she can have visitors. That will give us enough time to monitor her vitals and make sure she doesn't have any problems with the medication."

She hated to wait any longer, but she also didn't want to do anything that might jeopardize her condition, so Gloria begrudgingly agreed, along with her father. He and Amy returned to the waiting room as the doctor left to tend to his patients, but Gloria and Lloyd remained in the empty corridor. When he opened his arms, she rushed into his comforting embrace...and finally let go of her tears.

* * * *

Lloyd shifted uncomfortably in the back seat of the taxi for the hundredth time. No matter how long he lived, he would never understand why the English loved their modes of transportation. The seats were lumpy, the radio was too loud, and cigarette smoke seeped from every nook and cranny.

As the driver came to a screeching halt in front of the hospital, he hurriedly paid the man his fee just so he could escape. When he drove away, Lloyd smoothed the creases in his clothing and sighed as he did what he could to look presentable. If only the hospital wasn't so far from home. He would gladly have traded the taxi for his horse and the hard seat on his wagon – splinters and all.

Lloyd took a deep breath and walked toward the entrance. It had been two days since his future mother-in-law's stroke, and hopefully she would be able to leave the hospital by the weekend, if she continued improving. He hoped she was on the mend, because he could tell Gloria was in need of some much-needed rest.

He felt helpless as he watched her struggling to make sure everyone's needs were met. Her undying faithfulness toward her family and friends was just one of the many reasons he fell in love with her, but he could discern by the look in her eyes that her strength was slowly waning. It made his heart ache to see her moping around with the weight of the world on her shoulders, but there was little he could do besides make sure she and her family were taken care of. Ruth's healing was up to God in His own time.

Lloyd pushed open the heavy door that led to the stairway, opting to climb the stairs to the third floor instead of taking the elevator. It took longer to get there, but he learned quickly that it was the easier route, after being crammed in the tiny elevator with several other visitors, like sardines in a tin can.

When he reached the third floor, he was surprised to find Gloria leaning against the wall outside her mother's room. Her arms were crossed over her chest, and she was aimlessly shuffling her feet against the cold tile floor. Seeing her sad expression made his pulse race, as he automatically started thinking the worst. He quickened his steps to reach her side, and Gloria looked up and smiled at him when she noticed him approaching.

"Is something wrong?" he asked.

She shook her head as she laced her arm through his and motioned for him to walk with her along the hallway. "Bishop Paul and his wife are visiting with mother and father right now, and I told them I would wait outside."

They walked in silence for a while, until they reached a small waiting room at the end of the hall. Gloria went inside and took a seat by the large window that overlooked the hospital parking lot. Thankfully, the room was empty, so they could have a few minutes of privacy. Lloyd leaned over and gently kissed her cheek before sitting in the chair beside her.

"How is she doing?"

Gloria gazed longingly out the window and attempted a smile. "She had trouble sleeping last night, but she was able to take a long nap around noon, so she's feeling better than she was. Her appetite has returned too, so that's a good thing."

He nodded as he waited for her to continue.

"The medicine is working, but she's still going to need physical therapy, and the doctor suggested moving her to a swing bed in the nursing home next door once she's discharged from the hospital."

Lloyd furrowed a brow at her answer, but it did make sense, especially with them living so far from downtown Lancaster.

"I'm just afraid we won't be able to pay for it all. They put some money away in savings, but I don't know if it will be enough..."

Lloyd turned in his seat and grabbed her hands to keep her from continuing. "*Neh*...don't do that. If we need to, we'll talk to the elders of the church about having a fundraiser to help pay for the medical bills. There are some things you just can't help, Gloria. God allowed your mother's life to be spared, and that's all that matters right now."

She smiled, but it was a half-hearted smile, at best. "How is Amy doing? Is she behaving for Mrs. Graber?"

Lloyd chuckled as he thought back to earlier in the day when he spotted Amy playing in their next-door neighbor's yard with one of her pets. "*Yah*, she's fine. The Graber's have two dogs, three cats, and several ducks, so she may never want to come home again."

Gloria grinned at his remark, and this time he could tell it was genuine. It made his heart swell seeing how close she and Amy were, especially since he had no siblings of his own. Even though Gloria was nineteen years old and Amy was just eight, the age difference never caused a problem. If anything, it made their bond stronger.

"Would you be angry if we have to postpone the wedding?" she asked.

Lloyd stopping caressing her hand and gave her a curious look. "*Neh*, but why would we have to do that? Her doctor said she should be doing much better by Thanksgiving."

Gloria looked out the window again, and when she spoke, her voice was low and barely audible. "But what if she isn't? There's no way my father can take care of her and Amy and continue working every day. I can't just desert him if he needs me."

She said it with conviction, but there was an underlying sadness that was unmistakable. Of course, he would never ask her to leave her family during their time of need, but he also couldn't deny the resentment he felt over her having to make such a sacrifice. He knew he would do the same thing if the situation was reversed, but nevertheless, it left a big hole in his heart knowing they may have to wait even longer to get married.

"We'll just have to continue praying for your mother's healing. This is in God's hands – not ours. All we can do it take it one day at a time."

Lloyd raised one of her hands to his mouth and tenderly kissed it, which brought fresh tears to her eyes. Before they had the chance to escape, he stood and helped her to her feet. "Let's go see if the Bishop and his wife are still here."

She didn't argue with him, and as they made their way into the corridor, Lloyd held fast to her hand, not caring if it was a bold move for such a public place. He loved the woman by his side, and they were engaged to be married. If he wanted to hold her hand in public, then he would do it and not think twice about who might be watching.

They walked in silence to her mother's room, and when Gloria gently rapped on the door, he heard a faint welcome from inside. As they entered the room, they were greeted by Bishop Paul, his wife, and Gloria's father, who stood by Ruth's bedside.

"You arrived just in time to pray with us," he said.

As they gathered around Ruth's bed and joined hands, Bishop Paul delivered a powerful and uplifting prayer for her continued healing and a blessing upon her family. Lloyd opened his eyes and stole a glance beside him at Gloria, and he felt a pang in his heart when he saw the tears streaming down her beautiful face. Oh, what he wouldn't give to be able to snap his fingers and take away her worry and fears.

If only it were that easy.

* * * *

Gloria sat up straight in the recliner, gasping for breath. Her pillow and blanket fell into a heap on the floor as she reached over and switched on the overhead light, trying not to wake her mother in the process. She took a couple of deep breaths, letting the rhythmic beeping of her mother's heartrate monitor calm her rattled nerves.

She couldn't recall the exact details of the horrible dream that woke her from a deep sleep, but she did remember the sensation of falling. Every time she tried to grasp on to something to break her fall, it would slip through her fingers and send her plummeting even faster. Gloria placed a hand over her heart and closed her eyes. It was the middle of the night and she could faintly hear the nurses talking outside their door. They were nearing day four of her mother's hospital stay, but thankfully the doctor agreed to return and sign her discharge papers around noon.

Gloria was looking forward to sleeping in her own bed again. The recliner wasn't fit for napping, much less sleeping an entire night, and she couldn't get comfortable on the sofa bed in the room either. She understood now what the phrase "cabin fever" meant, and she didn't like it one bit.

She opened her eyes and looked out the window at the full moon dangling high above the trees. She just wanted to go home – to her own bed, her own pillow, and her own blanket.

"Penny for your thoughts."

She turned to find her mother pressing a button on the remote beside her bed that would raise her into a sitting position. Gloria stood so she could fluff the pillows behind her mother's back and kiss her wrinkled cheek.

"I don't think they would be worth that much," she replied.

Her mother smiled, which fueled Gloria's hope for a full recovery. She'd come so far since being admitted to the hospital. In the beginning, she couldn't smile due to the paralysis on her left side, but she was improving a little bit more every day. It was a small grin, but it was there, and that's what counted.

"You've been tossing and turning all night. What's wrong?" she asked.

Gloria felt her cheeks flush. "I'm so sorry. I didn't mean to keep you awake."

Her mother patted the bed and carefully inched her way to the far side. "Come here and tell me what's going on with you."

Gloria smiled, recalling the many times she'd crawled into her parent's bed in the early morning hours after waking from a bad dream. Her mother would hold her in her arms, and they would lay there and talk until the sun came up, always keeping their voices to a low whisper so as not to wake her father.

Gloria pushed down the bed's side rail and laid down beside her mother, who in turn snuggled her inside the thick blanket covering her hospital bed. She thought it might feel awkward, especially now that she was a grown woman, but it was the soothing balm she desperately needed to steady her nerves.

"Now...tell me what's on your mind," her mother said.

Gloria frowned, realizing there would be no way to get out of the conversation she dreaded.

"I've been trying to come up with a way to help dad with his farrier business, so he can spend more time with you once you're moved to the swing bed at the nursing home. Lloyd said he would work longer hours to get caught up on dad's orders, and Mrs. Graber agreed to watch Amy for me while I help him. She also said she and Mr. Graber could take turns driving Amy to school during the week..."

Her mother waved a hand in the air to stop her from saying anything further. "Hold on. What are you talking about?" she asked.

Gloria furrowed a brow as she turned slightly so she could see her mother's face. Even by the dim glow of the full moon shining through the window she could tell by the look on her face that she was genuinely confused, which surprised her.

"It's okay, mom. Lloyd and I have already talked about this, and we've decided to postpone our wedding for the time being. Right now, I just want to make sure you, dad, and Amy are taken care of."

Her mother didn't respond for several minutes, which worried her, but when she heard her sniffling behind her, it suddenly dawned on her she was crying.

"I'm sorry. Did I say something wrong?" she asked.

Her mother hugged her tightly against her body. "*Neh*, my sweet angel, you said everything right. I love that you want to take care of us, but your father and I have this worked out. What you need to focus on is your wedding."

Now Gloria was the one confused.

"Your aunt Janine volunteered to help us, and she'll be flying in from Ohio tomorrow afternoon. She'll stay with me during the day and help with my physical therapy while your father works, and then he'll stay with me during the night while she watches over you and Amy. She'll take Amy to school on her way to the nursing home, and your father will pick her up in the afternoon. Sheriff Hawkins said he would drive Janine and your father to and from the hospital as often as he could to help us save money on taxi fees."

Gloria smiled for the first time since her mother's incident, and the relief that instantly flooded her body almost brought her to tears.

"I had no idea your sister was coming to help," she replied. "I haven't seen her in ages."

Her mother laughed, softly.

"I haven't either," she said. "I'll need your help cooking meals for Amy and your father while Janine is with me during the day, but that's it. I want you to stop fretting over us and keep planning your wedding. Have you and Lloyd settled on a date?"

Gloria sat up and spun around on the bed so she could face her mother while talking to her. "*Yah*, we thought about the week of Thanksgiving, but if that's too soon we can wait until the week after Christmas."

Her mother shook her head. "*Neh*, I want you to plan for Thanksgiving. That's two months from now, and it will give me a goal to work toward during my physical therapy."

Her determination to get better warmed her heart, and as she leaned over and kissed her cheek, she felt excited for the first time in days, and she couldn't wait to talk to Lloyd and start planning their wedding again.

Gloria and her mother talked until the sun peeked over the horizon, and when her father returned to the hospital later that morning, she could barely contain her happiness. Everything was starting to fall into place, and she knew it was all because of God's grace and mercy. He was the only reason her mother was alive and getting better each day. He provided a way for her aunt Janine to help them in their time of need, and He would continue helping her all the way to the alter on her wedding day and beyond.

"You've been cooped up in this hospital too long," her mother remarked. "Go home. Spend some time with Lloyd. Get some rest."

She didn't have to be told twice, and after hugging them both, she grabbed her things and raced for the elevator. She was bursting at the seams to see Lloyd and tell him the good news.

Rest would have to wait.

* * * *

Lloyd paced back and forth in the barn as Bella watched his every move. In all his life, he'd never met such an ornery animal. He tried once again to lift her front right leg so he could check her shoe, but she side-stepped him and grunted.

Lloyd bit his tongue and tried not to lose his temper. When he sat down on a stack of hay and crossed one ankle over the other, Bella never took her eyes off him. It was almost comical the way she avoided him like the plague.

"Okay, Bella. I'm going to say this one more time. I need to check that shoe, so you and I have got to come to some kind of a truce. What do you say?"

She threw her head back and whinnied, as if she understood, but when he heard a car pull into the Beller's driveway, he realized what she was really whinnying about. He shook his head and laughed as he pointed a finger at her snout. "We're not finished, so don't go anywhere."

Bella grunted again as Lloyd made his way to the side door of the barn, but as he reached for the handle, the door swung open, revealing Gloria on the other side. She was breathing heavily, as if she'd run home from the hospital, and he would've panicked if she didn't have such an enormous grin on her face.

"Hey you..."

The words had barely passed his lips before she was flying into his arms, nearly knocking him off his feet. He wrapped his arms around her waist and grabbed the door frame to keep them both from tumbling to the ground. "Whoa! What's this about?" he asked.

She squeezed him so hard he could barely breathe, and when she finally loosened her grip, he took a step back and massaged his sore ribs while attempting to take a deep breath.

"I'm so sorry," she laughed. "Did I hurt you?"

He grasped her arm and pulled her inside the barn so he could close the door. "I'm okay. What are you doing here? I was planning on coming to the hospital around noon, but Bella is being a diva again."

They both looked her way, but Bella snorted at them and walked in the opposite direction, which made them laugh.

"I was ordered to come home and get some rest."

Lloyd moved a long lock of hair away from her eyes and laced it over her ear before brushing his fingertips against her cheek. "I think that's a great idea. You look tired, and you need a good night's sleep."

Gloria took his hand and brought it to her lips. "I will, but right now I want to talk about our wedding."

Lloyd's heart sank. She looked so happy, but he just couldn't bring himself to talk about their postponed wedding again – not when he knew in the end it would only sadden them both.

"Gloria..."

She shook her head. "*Neh*...it's okay. Mom and I spent most of the night talking, and she told me to start planning it again because she and dad worked out a way for someone else to stay with her while she's in the nursing home."

Lloyd gave her a skeptical look. He was afraid to get his hopes up, but he could tell she was serious.

"My mom's sister, Janine, is flying in from Ohio, and she and dad are going to take turns staying with her. I'll explain more later, but the important thing is we can start making plans again. Mom wants us to keep our Thanksgiving date too. She said it would give her something to work toward while she's in physical therapy."

Lloyd was so happy and relieved he didn't know how to respond.

"God has been good to us," she continued. "He brought mom through this terrible ordeal, and I know He's going to take her the rest of the way until she's completely healed."

He intertwined his fingers with hers and led her over to the stack of hay so they could sit down.

"I couldn't agree with you more, and I have some good news to share too. Bishop Paul told me yesterday there's going to be an auction in a couple of weeks to help raise money to pay off your mother's medical bills. He's planning some other fundraising events too."

He noticed the corners of her eyes swell with tears, and she remained quiet for a long time before leaning over and tenderly pressing her lips against his. "God has truly blessed us," she whispered.

Lloyd kissed her forehead and pulled her close so she could rest her head on his shoulder. "*Yah*, He certainly has."

The peace and quiet surrounding them was interrupted by the sound of horse hooves on the ground close to them. Before Lloyd could turn his head, Bella was sidling up next to him and pushing her snout against his arm.

"I think she's trying to apologize for her behavior," Gloria remarked with a grin.

Lloyd chuckled as he rubbed under Bella's chin. "Are you going to let me look at that shoe now?"

Bella shook her head and whinnied loudly before walking away again.

"Okay," Gloria said. "Maybe I was wrong."

Lloyd nuzzled his mouth against her ear and laughed. Oh, how he couldn't wait to make this beautiful woman his bride. With any luck, the time would pass quickly so they could look forward to spending the rest of their lives together as husband and wife.

His greatest wish would soon become his reality...a definite dream come true.

AMISH VALLEY

MICHELLE BENTON

<u>**January**</u>

You have to stop this! Naomi chided herself, trying to silence what was happening in her head. But she could not stop her foot from tapping and her neck from bopping as she hummed under her breath. *Someone is going to catch you one day and then you'll have some explaining to do.*

She kept her head down so she would not be heard laughing. However, her snickers did not fall on deaf ears and when she turned her head from the firewood she was splitting, two of the women glared at her from their various vegetables.

"Do you find something amusing, Naomi?" Anke Hilty asked coldly but Naomi quickly shook her head and averted her eyes. Still, she could not stop the smile from toying on her generous mouth. She had only been welcomed into the district four months earlier but it seemed that Naomi was still regarded as Englisch to several of the women in the community. Naomi was smart enough to realize that it had little to do with her personally and more to do with upsetting tradition but it did not ease her sense of discomfort. Women like Anke and Anke's sister, Emma made the conversion to the Amish way of life difficult sometimes. If not for Naomi's unstoppable sense of humor, she was sure she would have returned to life in Indianapolis long ago. *I'll be an outsider until I get baptized,* she reasoned, turning her attention fully toward the garden now and forcing any other "English" thought from her head...like the popular song which had been playing over and over in her mind since she had woken at dawn.

"Naomi, you can't be serious!" her mother had screamed when Naomi had told of her plans to convert. "You can't go a day without the internet!"

Naomi had shaken her head, expecting the histrionics from her mother, inwardly relieved to know she would not have to listen to the woman's incessant shrieking day in and day out.

"I can and I will."

"We won't be able to visit you!" her father had protested. "They don't allow for outsiders in their community."

"I know! Isn't it wonderful?" As Naomi spoke, she genuinely meant the words. The Amish way of life, their seclusion, their devotion to each other and God was inspirational to her in every conceivable way.

But it had been Stephen who had almost made her change her mind.

"You can't run away from your problems by disappearing, sis," he told her. "You will just find yourself walking into a whole new whack of problems. But if this is what you want to do, I support you, no matter what. I hope you know I'll miss you."

His words had hit a sour note with Naomi and that night and every night subsequently, what he had said had rung in her head. *I am not running away,* she told herself over and over. *I am trying to under-complicate my very overcomplicated life. It is too messy now, filled with things I do not require. All I need is to surround myself with fresh air, hard work and true, unpretentious, like minded people.* She knew that her family was concerned about her mental state. Ever since her fiancé, Carlos had fled town with her best friend, things had begun to spiral downhill for Naomi. In the aftermath of the betrayal, she had set fire to all his belongings during an onset of uncontrollable fury. She had done so on the front lawn of the house they shared, hoping that Carlos would return and see a pile of ash where his beloved Gucci ties had once been. Carlos had never shown his face at the house again and unfortunately, the act had resulted in an arrest as the flame had spread, damaging the neighbor's car. She had been lucky, let off on probation as it was a first offense and then promptly fired from her job as a personal support worker.

"I'm sorry, Arry, I really am," her boss had told her, regret gleaming in his eyes. "But you can't have an arson record and work with the public, especially not in the medical field."

"I've been working here for four years! It was a stupid act of passion!" Naomi had protested, tears threatening to flow down her round cheeks as her full mouth quivered. "I am no danger to anyone!"

"I know that, Arry and you know that but you know you are required to have a clean record. I can't keep you employed with this agency any more." As he led her away in full blown sobs, he emptily promised to give her an excellent reference but he knew just as well as she did that no one was ever going to hire her again as a PSW. A felony was a felony after all. From there, she had been evicted as she wallowed in depression, eating ice cream and watching Netflix twenty hours a day. Naomi had not a cent in savings and between asking her parents for money and living on the streets, Naomi opted for the latter. She went to stay with Stephen for a short time before having an epiphany one day at the farmer's market; she would join the Amish. At the start, even she had recognized how obscure an idea it was but it did not stop her from investigating. She began frequenting the market more often, discovering that it was almost unheard of for outsiders to convert. Naomi pushed the issue, finding only two people who would entertain her questions. One was a man named Camp Girod, a solemn faced farmer who answered her inquiries in as few words as possible but Naomi soon learned that was his way of speaking and not rudeness. The other was Emma Hilty, a girl who had promised to become a fruitful friendship but had somehow fallen short down the line. Both had seemed happy that she had shown so much interest in their faith and were eager to educate her to the best of their ability. One afternoon, Camp brought the bishop of their district to meet with Naomi to answer some things they did not know. Naomi had almost hugged the tall, shy man but immediately stopped herself. *You must behave like a proper Amish woman from here on in,* Naomi told herself. *No more city girl shenanigans.*

The bishop initially had not been convinced by Naomi but as time went on, he began to recognize her intentions as true and slowly, with

Camp and Emma whispering praise in his ear, he eventually began to take her seriously.

"It is often very difficult for an outsider to simply assimilate into our culture. We don't have the luxuries which your kind seem to deem necessity to function," the Bishop had warned. "More often than not, the English return to the life in which they have been reared."

"That won't happen with me, Bishop!" Naomi declared with conviction. "I will be one hundred and twenty-five percent committed to the community. You'll see!"

The elderly man had raised a bushy eyebrow, somewhat distastefully at Naomi's loud proclamation.

"Naomi, in our community, patience and peace are considered large attributes. The quick tempered and moody do not fare well in our lifestyle," Bishop Kurtz continued. "We are one with God's teaching and he teaches the virtues of the meek. Do you believe you can follow those teachings?"

Naomi nodded eagerly although inwardly she cringed at her own lie. In truth, she had little religious teachings and knew very little about the Bible. She vowed that she would read the scripture from start to finish. *I'll do it in one sitting if that's what it takes!* In the end, Bishop Kurtz decided that Naomi would try the Amish way, largely influenced by Camp and Emma's convincing but partially enthralled by her belief that she was meant to be Amish. Under normal circumstances, the Bishop would not have entertained such an inane idea but Naomi had become a legend in the district and he had finally allowed his curiosity to get the best of him. Every evening after market, one of the parishioners would regale the bishop of tales. A young, bubbly woman would stop by their stalls at the market, begging for information about their culture. Most dismissed her, believing her to be a reporter and not wishing to fraternize with outsiders or disclose anything inappropriate. However, Emma had been amused by her tenacity and began to converse with the girl. She had been pleasantly surprised to discover that Naomi had a genuine desire to forsake the outside world and start fresh within the security of their community. Before long, Camp Girod, whose dairy booth neighbored Emma's meat display, heard the outgoing Naomi and found himself drawn into conversations also. If Emma and Camp had not been such upstanding members of the district, Bishop Kurtz would have never met Naomi Pryce. In the end, however, he was just as smitten with the girl as the other two members of his parish.

On a warm night in September, Naomi, in only a very simply skirt and white blouse, said good bye to Indianapolis and moved into the Hilty's home in rural Indiana with Bishop Kurtz's blessing.

That had been four months earlier. In that time, Emma had lost her good nature with Naomi. Naomi suspected it had much to do with the fact that Anke did not like her. Naomi tried to tell herself it did not matter, that she belonged there just as much as they did. *Just because I wasn't born into this life, doesn't make me any less Amish!* She pep talked herself. At that moment, another popular song blasted into her head. She shook her head mournfully. *My own psyche is mocking me.*

"It's raining on your head, Naomi and yet you seem so content, sitting there in the mud." Naomi whipped her head up and looked at the speaker. Anke and Emma's brother Evan stood above her, his light blue eyes twinkling with laughter. To her surprise, she realized he was right. The sunlight had disappeared and dark rain clouds had overtaken the sky. She suddenly realized that the Hilty sisters had retreated inside without saying a word. Water was seeping into her boots and the air had taken on a sudden chill. She rubbed her hands against her

"Come inside before you fall ill," Evan laughed, offering a hand. She eagerly accepted and followed the oldest Hilty sibling inside the farmhouse. Anke scowled at them from the window and Naomi realized she was still holding Evan's hand. Embarrassed, she pulled her palm from his and he turned, winking at her. Naomi blushed crimson. Evan had bestowed endless attention upon her since her arrival in the district. From the first night, he had told her stories on the porch and introduced her around to the neighbors. In turn, he asked that she tell him about the city, the sights and people. Naomi did her best to make it sound exciting, despite her recollection being less than glamorous but it seemed the more she embellished, the more captivated Evan became. Naomi had almost felt like he had claimed her but of course that was ridiculous. That was something the English would do, not the gentle-minded Amish. Still, Naomi was flattered and relished the friendship she found in Evan.

"Let me make some tea. You should change your clothes. I don't understand how you can be so at peace in the rain," Evan told her. "Especially someone so accustom to having warmth at their fingertips!"

Naomi shrugged. It was difficult not to be at peace in such surroundings. There was no bustle, no stress. The days were long, yes, but Naomi felt as if she had always been tilling fields and saying prayers. She hadn't been certain that the religious aspect would appeal to her, being reared nearly agnostic but the more time she had spent in worship, hearing God's plans, the more Naomi recognized what she had been missing from her life. *You made the right choice coming here,* she told herself as she quickly changed and brushed out her dark hair. She regarded her reflection in the mirror. She was an attractive woman by any standards; shoulder length straight brown hair, her bangs finally growing out from the blunt cut she had worn from before joining the community. Her dark eyes were intelligent and wide, her mouth constantly curved to a smile. Her inner happiness radiated outwardly and she found herself smiling in the glass.

"Are you coming?" Evan bellowed from downstairs. "The tea is becoming cold!"

"Yes!" Naomi yelled back and winced. *You need to tone it down!*

She hurried out of her small room and down the stairs to meet with Evan in the kitchen. Emma stopped her, stepping out from the shadows in the sitting room.

"Naomi," she said in a low voice. Naomi paused in surprise, glancing toward the kitchen but Evan was not standing there.

"You need to stay away from my brother," she warned. "Don't say I didn't warn you." Naomi felt her heart skip a beat. In the darkness of the hall, Naomi thought she saw a glint of anger in the younger girl's eyes. She did not reply, instead backing away, looking hurt at Emma's words, watching the younger girl disappear up the stairs. *I suppose I am not good enough for her brother, then? Am I always going to be an outsider? Will they never accept me here?*

"Naomi, would you care to take a walk with me after supper tomorrow?" Camp asked conversationally after worship. Naomi nodded.

"Of course," she replied, unsuspectingly. "I would love to!"

"There is a matter I would like to discuss with you," he said in his usual somber tone. Naomi smiled to herself but nodded again. She could not imagine Camp being anything but serious. *He probably wants to discuss the winter frost and he makes it sound like the world is about to come to an end,* she thought jokingly. She dared not jest with Camp. He was far too routine for such play. Naomi had once been present when Camp had been unwell and overslept as a result. She had never seen anyone so flustered in all her life. His entire demeanor had been altered and he snapped viciously at everyone in his wake. Naomi had been wounded by his sharp tones until Emma had told her that Camp was the most structured person in their district. From the time he was a child, he had risen with the roosters and planned every single minute of every day down to the second. When his schedule was disrupted, it made him confused and disoriented. After learning that, Naomi had gone out of her way to accommodate his whims. After all, if it had not been for Camp, she likely would never have been allowed in the community. Naomi owed him a debt of gratitude. Also, Camp was one of her only friends. She didn't know why, but Camp seemed to like her.

"You're not like anyone I would ever imagine Camp Giron associating," Anke told Naomi icily one day after Camp walked away. Naomi and he had been speaking over the fence for almost half an hour. Naomi had raised an eyebrow, stung by the connotation.

"And why not?" she demanded. "I am just as God fearing and hard working as anyone here, Anke! I wish you wouldn't imply that I'm not!"

"Maybe so," the older sister had replied. "But you are also the loudest. Camp is a quiet, gentle man. You are so...brash."

"Brash? I am not brash!" Naomi had yelled. Anke had smiled thinly as if to say "I rest my case." Naomi had gone out of her way to avoid speaking with Anke after that but Anke made it easy. She barely had two words to say to Naomi under the best of circumstances. Inwardly, though, she wondered what Camp found interesting about her. *Anke is not wrong. I am exactly the opposite of the man. I always thought that introverts found extroverts exhausting.* Naomi did not have to wait long to find out.

The following evening, the night had turned bitterly cold but after supper, Camp knocked on the Hilty door. Naomi hurried threw on her coat, scarf and gloves before adjusting her bonnet and heading toward the front door to meet her friend. Evan grabbed her by the arm as she went to leave the kitchen, a scowl darkening his fair face.

"Are you going out walking with Camp Giron?" he demanded. Surprised, Naomi nodded at the question.

"Yes," she answered, cocking her head in confusion. Evan's blue eyes narrowed dangerously.

"Is that a problem?" Naomi asked nervously. She studied his face for an answer and suddenly he realized how tightly he was holding her. Abruptly, he let her go, shame flooding his face.

"No, of course not," he told her hastily. "I – it's very cold outside is all. Please dress well." With that he disappeared into the back of the house, leaving Naomi staring after him, open mouthed. *Am I delusional or was that an act of jealousy?* She asked herself, a warm glow of happiness filling her insides. She had suspected that Evan liked her but he had never been anything more than friendly toward her even though the community called his ways flirty. She secretly hoped that he was jealous of Camp. She pushed Evan out of her mind as she remembered that Camp was waiting for her. *You must not make Camp wait,* she thought guiltily but Camp did not look perturbed as he stood in the foyer, chatting with Mrs. Hilty.

"Ah, there you are, Naomi. Please do not be late. We have a very busy morning tomorrow," the matriarch ordered and Naomi nodded obligingly. Naomi had never given the Hilty's any cause for alarm. She had done everything per her agreement with Bishop Kurtz.

"Remember, Naomi," Bishop Kurtz had told her when she had arrived. "It is not what I expect of you but what God and this community expect of you. You will see a reflection of yourself in every action, good or bad. The choice is yours but in the end, it is only you who must answer to God."

"Shall we?" Camp extended his arm and Naomi took it, smiling. The pathway to the road was icy and Camp held fast to her as she almost slipped several times.

"My goodness, Camp," Naomi exclaimed as ten minutes had only seen them a few hundred feet down the road. "Perhaps we should plan our walk for another night."

"I would prefer not to, Naomi if you do not mind indulging me." Naomi smiled and shrugged tolerantly. She could barely feel her face or toes in the extreme cold but she did not want to disappoint Camp.

"This sounds urgent, Camp. Of course, we can speak tonight. What is going on?"

Camp paused and looked down at her, his own dark eyes soulfully deep. He seemed to be thinking about his words and in spite of her resolve to be patient, Naomi wished he would spit it out. She flexed her fingers inside her gloves to ensure they were still there.

"Naomi, I am very proud of the way you have situated yourself in the community," he began. She smiled, abashed by the praise.

"I couldn't have done it without you, Camp. You know that, right?"

"I believe that your perseverance would have paid off regardless of my small role. However, I am happy you are here."

"I am thrilled to be here!" she announced. He nodded soberly and cocked his head.

"Have you given any thought to your baptism?" he questioned.

"Bishop Kurtz has suggested April. Personally, I would like to do it tomorrow but I confess, I never much wanted to join the Polar Bear Club." A look of confusion passed over Camp's eyes and Naomi realized he didn't understand the reference. *You really need to get your head out of the English,* she scolded herself again.

"Anyway, you'll know when I know. I'm pretty sure everyone around here gets an invite, right? Is that what you want to talk about? You're worried I might go back to the city after everything you've done to bring me here?" she asked, smiling. Camp's brow furrowed and Naomi realized that he had not entertained that thought whatsoever, at least not until she had brought it up.

"No..." he said slowly. "That was not what I wanted to speak to you regarding."

He said nothing and Naomi felt a smidgen of annoyance. *I know patience is a virtue but I'm becoming an ice sculpture here!*

"Camp, you're my friend, you know that, right?" He nodded, seemingly more confused by the conversation shift.

"As my friend, probably my best friend here, I am begging you to ask me whatever it is because I am freezing to death! I swear there are corpses warmer than me right now!"

Camp inhaled sharply and nodded.

"I wanted to ask you, if, once you get baptized..."

"Yes?"

"If you would consider giving me your hand in marriage?"

<u>April</u>

"Welcome, Naomi Pryce to our community!"

A cheer erupted and Naomi, soaked to her knickers, beamed at the crowd which surrounded her. She noted with pride that even Anke nodded in approval, a thin, funny smile pursing her lips. *I am one of them now! Finally! They can't call me an outsider anymore!* She thought. She turned to Bishop Kurtz and bowed slightly in thanks.

"We are pleased to have you, Naomi. You have demonstrated the loyalty, hard work and patience which we value so highly. If only you would work on your Pennsylvania Dutch..." A small chuckle flew through the group and Evan lunged forward to take her arm.

"Everyone speaks English anyway, *liebchen*. Come on, Arry. Let's eat!" Happily, she allowed herself to be led toward the Hilty barn where a feast had been set up for the baptism. Out of the corner of her eye, she saw Camp standing alone, under a tree, looking forlorn.

Since the frigid night of their walk, Camp had not come calling and Naomi admitted that she missed his company terribly. Of course, Evan was her constant companion, joking and laughing with her, despite the tongue wagging of the community.

"She does not behave properly," some of the older women complained. "She flirts recklessly with the Hilty boy and she lives in that house!"

"He is no better," others countered. "He has been brought up right in this community and he blatantly disregards our traditions. He acts like he has English blood."

But neither Evan or Naomi seemed to mind the gossip. It was not because they did not hear of it; in fact, Mr. and Mrs. Hilty often forbade them to be together alone but they still managed to find a way to see one another and enjoy each other's company. Naomi had been counting the days to her christening. She knew that the moment she officially became Amish, Evan would ask her to marry. *I wonder if he will do it today even,* Naomi thought, peering at him out of the corner of her eye. He returned her look of adoration and impulsively squeezed her hand, not releasing it. Naomi did not take her palm away this time, despite the looks she received from the members. She could almost hear their thoughts; *she just got accepted into the fold and look at her! Acting like a fallen woman!* Naomi did not care. She was incredibly happy and she knew she was about to become happier.

The day progressed beautifully. There was food and banter. The only dark cloud was Camp's almost palpable sadness. She had not outright refused his pre-emptive proposal but she had let him down in a way that he knew she did not see a future with him. *Camp will find someone. He is dependable and hardworking. Any woman in the community would be lucky to have him.* But the thoughts did not alleviate Naomi's guilt and she forced herself to focus on the festivities. As the afternoon wound into evening, she found herself exhausted. The events of the day had taken a toll on her and she wanted to retire early for the evening. She excused herself just after dark and retreated to her bedroom. As she lay in bed, a smile touching her lips, she knew that tomorrow would be the day Evan would ask her to marry him.

"Naomi!" She bolted up in her bed, scared out of a dream state. It took her a moment to reconcile her surroundings and then, through the dark, she peered at Emma and Anke who stood in the doorway, both relief and anger written on their faces.

"What?" she croaked, her throat like cotton. "What happened?"

Emma exhaled slowly and crept into the dark room, clutching a letter in her hand.

"You're still here."

"Well I almost jumped out of my skin but yes, I am still here. What is going on?" Naomi demanded, throwing her legs over the side of the twin bed and rubbing her eyes.

"We thought you had gone with him," Anke answered crisply, also entering the room. She snatched the paper out of Emma's hand and flung it at Naomi.

"Gone with who? Guys, it's a little early in the morning for brain teasers. Can you tell me what is happening or can I go back to bed?"

"Do you know anything about this?"

Naomi picked up the single sheet of paper and read the note scrawled on the blank canvas.

Dear *Daed, Mammi,* Anke and Emma,

You have always done your best for me but I have never felt like I belonged in this community. I think I always knew that I would leave at some point but it wasn't until Naomi came that I knew the world was calling me. I could not stop thinking about the places she told me, the foods she had eaten, the people she met. I could not understand why she would give that all up to live here, in this boring, judgemental place. I have gone to the city. Don't worry about me, please. I am sure I will make my way just fine. I know this comes as a disappointment but I could not bear the thought of spending my life farming. I love you all.

Yours Always,

Evan

P.S. Tell Naomi if she changes her mind to come and find me in Indianapolis.

Slowly, Naomi read and reread the letter until tears began to slip down her cheeks and blot the ink on the paper. Anke grabbed it and swatted the water from the page scowling.

"*Mamm* and *Daed* haven't read it yet, Naomi. Don't ruin it. You've already ruined enough around here." Anke spun on her heel and stormed out the door, leaving Emma behind. The younger sister looked at Naomi's devastated face and gently placed her hand upon her shoulder.

"I told you to stay away from Evan," she murmured. "Not because you're not good enough for him but because he is not good enough for you."

<u>May</u>

"Naomi, you have been moping around here for a month now. I miss your sunny smile," Bishop Kurtz told her one day as he passed by the farm.

"I am not moping, Bishop!" Naomi protested. "I am working!"

"Yes, yes you are working and doing a fine job, I might add," he agreed. "But you need to forget about Evan. I understand you were very fond of him."

"He was my friend." Naomi dropped the hoe and stared at the bishop. The look was enough to stop him from uttering his next thoughts but his eyes travelled over her head to look at something in the distance.

"Well, I still miss your smile, child," he told her. "And sometimes when God closes a door, he opens up a window." She followed his gaze as he turned to leave and she saw Camp approaching in a wagon.

"Good day, Naomi," Camp greeted, somewhat nervously. "Would you care to go for a ride? I have an appointment with a medical doctor in town today."

Immediately, Naomi was concerned.

"Are you all right?" she asked, hurrying forward, wiping her dirty hands on her apron.

"Oh yes. Nothing serious. But I wouldn't mind the company," he replied. Naomi nodded quickly. *It is serious enough for him to ask her for companionship after an estrangement*, she thought nervously.

"Just give me a minute to change."

She was beside him in the carriage in minutes and they rode silently for a while.

"Naomi, when are you going to stop brooding about?"

"I am not brooding!" she snapped. *I'm not brooding! I am pining. Evan could come back any day. That is not brooding or moping. That is called being hopeful.*

"Fine." They continued their trip quietly. Naomi realized how unfair she was being to Camp. Camp was there. Evan was not. Camp stood by her. Evan hadn't even asked if she wanted to go with him. Why would she not give Camp a chance?

"I'm sorry, Camp," she finally said. He shot her a look out of the corner of his eye.

"What for?"

"I don't deserve your affections. You have been too good to me since the beginning."

"You are very worthy of all things good, Naomi. It has been my pleasure you call you my friend."

Naomi looked at him, his noble face proud and unsmiling.

"Would it be your pleasure to call me your wife?"

October

When their engagement was announced at worship, Naomi was met with genuine adulation.

"Camp Giron is a fine man. He will be Bishop one day, I promise you. You have made the right decision," Bishop Kurtz told her. "And I do believe you have made the man very happy. I have known Camp since he was a boy. I could count the amount of times he has smiled on one hand since then. Until you came along, Naomi. He adores you."

"He is a wonderful man," Naomi agreed, shooting her fiancé a look from across the salon. He met her gaze and smiled. Bishop Kurtz opened his mouth to say something else but seemed to reconsider.

"I hope you two will be very happy together, Naomi."

"I hope so too," she replied, a sudden stab of sadness overwhelming her. She would be lying to herself to say she didn't still think of Evan. She wondered if he was faring well in the city and if he ever thought about her. She knew that he wasn't coming back.

"He would not be welcome here if he did," Anke spat when Naomi asked her about him one night. Naomi had been shocked at the venom attached to his sister's words. Later, Emma pulled her aside.

"I know you were rather fond of my brother," Emma told her. "But there are many things you did not know about him."

Naomi arched an eyebrow. She wasn't sure she wanted to hear anything negative about Evan but curiosity got the better of her.

"Such as?" But Emma pursed her lips together as if she had already said too much.

"Just believe me, Naomi. You are marrying a good man in Camp. He will always do right by you." The words meant little to Naomi who lay awake at night, listening for sounds, dreaming that Evan would sneak back into the house and into her life again.

November

"You are a lovely bride," Emma whispered, adjusting the wreath of flowers about Naomi's head. Naomi smiled genuinely and gave her a hug.

"I don't think I've ever thanked you for all you've done for me, Emma," she told the younger girl. The blonde blinked and looked confused.

"What have I done?"

"You have helped give me a sense of community and family, one I have never had. I know you don't think I belong here but I want you to know that I care more about these people and our way of life than anyone or anything I have before in my life."

"I know you belong here, Naomi. That is why I asked Bishop Kurtz to speak with you. Camp and I saw the purity in your soul from the first day we met you. You are exactly the kind of person we want walking among us." The women smiled at each other and for the first time since Evan had left, Naomi felt truly happy. *I do belong here. I am one of them. Thanks to Emma and Bishop Kurtz. And thanks to Camp.*

"Shall we?" Emma offered Naomi her arm and the two made their way into the church where Camp stood waiting at the altar. Naomi felt like she was seeing him for the first time. He looked so handsome, his dark hair shining under his hat, two glossy curls hanging about his chiseled features. His eyes were alight with adoration as he watched his bride to be slowly walk toward him. His face broke into a beam so broad, Naomi was sure his face would crack from the force. Tears misted his irises. Emma gently squeezed her arm and released toward Camp. Suddenly, an abrupt gust of wind flew through the small chapel, extinguishing several of the lamps. Bride and groom turned to ward the entrance where a form stood, panting in the opened doorway.

"Evan!" Naomi gasped. Immediately, Mr. Hilty rose to his feet, his face crimson in anger.

"How dare you show your face in here!" he thundered.

"I am not here for you, *Daed*," Evan retorted, his eyes remaining on Naomi as he stumbled up the aisle.

"Naomi, don't marry him!" he called as he approached. "Come back to the city with me. I made a mistake leaving you here but you're all I can think about." A murmur flowed through the crowd. *He did think about me! He does miss me!* Naomi thought, dumbfounded. Evan was at the altar, grabbing for her hands, his blue eyes pleading.

"I'm sorry! I made a mistake," he said again, his mouth turning up into a smile of contrition. Naomi glanced up at Camp, who had lost the rare beam which had lit up the church. She looked at Emma who shook her head woefully and stared at her shoed. Her gaze shifted to Bishop Kurtz whose mouth had formed a fine line. She stared into the crowd and took in Evan's family's look of shame and fury. Then she looked back at Camp again.

"I'm sorry," she whispered at him and Camp hung his head in defeat, his shoulders visibly sagging. Evan tightened his grip on her hands and Naomi yanked them back, her eyes still trained on Camp.

"I am sorry," she said again, reaching up to wipe the tears falling onto his cheeks. "I am sorry that I ever made you hurt. I am so sorry that I wasted any time on this man. I am so terribly sorry that I ever doubted my future is in your arms. I love you, Camp." She turned furiously to Evan who had gone pale at Naomi's speech.

"But Naomi – "

"What kind of disgusting man claims to love a woman and leaves her for months only to barge in on her wedding? You're despicable, Evan. And you're not welcome in our community – my community! Get out and don't return." After a stunned second of silence, Evan whirled on his heel and ran out the door.

"And you don't even close the door behind you! Can you imagine marrying such a man?" Naomi yelled after him. Applause and laughter broke out and someone hurried to shut the double doors and relight the kerosene lamps. Naomi took Camp's hands in hers and they gazed into each other's eyes lovingly.

"Now, where were we?" she asked Bishop Kurtz without looking away.

END

BLOSSOMING AMISH

DEE DEE ROBBINS

Chapter One

Abigail Schroder awoke to the sound of birds chirping outside of her bedroom window.

Abigail took a deep breath and let out a sad sigh. Pulling herself up in bed, she propped her back against her pillow and watched as the birds worked side-by-side to craft a home for their future family.

While she generally loved to tiptoe over to the glass and watch as the pair of happy bluebirds worked together building a nest, this morning was different. Today their merry song only brought to mind her own misery.

The birds had always reminded her of what her future life would be like. She had dreamed of a life where she and her husband would work hand-in-hand to raise up a family in their Amish community.

Now, all of Abigail's dreams had been shattered.

"Jacob," she whispered the name gently, wishing that the past two months had been

nothing more than a dream.

Jacob had been her beau since the couple had met at a young people's gathering. For the past five years they had dated.

Abigail had planned to spend her entire life by Jacob's side. She had wanted to marry him, raise children with him, and then grow old along with him.

But now it was all gone.

She had been so hopeful the night Jacob had asked to see her alone. There had been something different about him. Rather than taking her to an Amish gathering or somewhere on a date, he told her that he just wanted to talk.

After five years together, Abigail could only imagine that he was going to ask for her to marry him. She had spent the entire day with a smile on her face as she did the regular chores of hanging laundry out to dry, scrubbing the floors, and helping her two younger sisters sew new dresses.

Abigail wasn't the only one who hoped for the best. Her fourteen-year-old sister Sally had begged her to tell her what happened first, and she had noticed a spark of excitement in her parents' eyes when Jacob arrived on his buggy.

She and Jacob had laughed together as they drove out to their favorite spot on the back of his *daed's* farm. Sitting together, they watched the sun go down while butterflies danced around them.

"Abigail," Jacob had whispered as she leaned her head against his shoulder and closed her eyes, "I have something I need to tell you."

It had been different than Abigail had expected. The words sounded wrong in her ears and, rather than seeming happy, Jacob's voice sounded strained.

She had looked up at him and watched as the man she had loved for so long forced a sad smile.

"I'm leaving, Abigail." He announced the words she had never expected to hear.

"Leaving?" She had repeated, "What do you mean?"

"I'm leaving the Amish," Jacob had announced with a shrug. When he looked down at her surprise he laughed, "Come on, girl. We've been together for five years. You knew it was going to happen eventually! I don't belong here! I'm not like anyone in the community and I don't want to be."

"Jacob," Abigail had tried to change his mind, "Our future..."

"Exactly," he had interrupted, "I want a future outside of a dirty chicken farm. I want to see the world. I want to be able to drive a car and wear normal clothes. I want to be able to talk on a phone and watch television without fear of getting in trouble. I want to be free, Abigail. I want to wipe the dirt of this place and these people off my hands. I want to try being whoever Jacob wants to be!"

"What about us?" Abigail's voice had sounded like no more than a whisper.

Jacob looked down and shook his head, "Abigail...there is no more us."

That had been it. Abigail had tried to convince him to stay with the Amish community, but all she could do was cry as he drove her home.

Even now, two months later, Abigail could hardly stop the tears from rolling down her cheeks as she watched the pair of birds working together outside of her window.

"Abigail," she heard her mother's familiar voice along with a soft rap against her bedroom door, "It's time to be up. Church will begin soon. I need your help with breakfast."

"Coming, Mom," Abigail managed to call out. She scooted down in bed and closed her eyes, trying to erase all her thoughts.

Church. If there was one place that she didn't want to go, it was church. Every two weeks the Amish community gathered in a different home to perform the service that started in the morning and ended with a group meal. Growing up, Abigail had loved the Sunday ritual, but now it was one of her least favorite parts of the week.

With the loss of Jacob, it felt as if Abigail had also lost all her faith in God. She had spend the last five years of her life so sure of her future, and now it felt that it had all been ripped away from her. And now, at twenty-three-years-old, Abigail found that she was one of the oldest singles in her Amish community. It appeared that her dream to be a wife and a mother was gone for good.

It seemed God no longer had a plan or a use for Abigail Schroder.

Chapter Two

While Abigail would rather have stayed home from church, she realized that this was not an option. Although her parents had been very understanding of her heartbreak, they were unyielding where church was concerned.

"God still has a plan for you, Abigail," her *mamm* would assure her any time that Abigail would mention her lack of spiritual fervor.

So, that Sunday morning, Abigail found herself squeezed onto one of the hard wooden benches in John Yoder's house. She glanced at her sisters, Sally and Emma, who sat on either side of her. They seemed completely engrossed in the message that the preacher was providing.

"I know the plans I have for you," The preacher was reading from the Bible, "Plans to prosper you and not to harm you, plans to give you a future and a hope."

Abigail shut her eyes and tried to will herself not to cry.

God no longer had a plan for her. She knew that. All her dreams had been erased when Jacob left. Life seemed completely pointless now and the future only dark and empty.

When the preacher had finished his message, the family joined the rest of the church for a large meal out in the barn. The Yoders had provided enough food for the entire congregation with baked chicken, homemade noodles, gravy, and potatoes. While she knew the food was delicious, Abigail could hardly force herself to eat.

As she shifted her food across her plate with her fork, she thought of services past. Services when Jacob had been by her side, amusing her with his funny stories from work and making her laugh at his constant antics. How she missed him!

"Abigail," she was brought out of her thoughts when her sister Emma gave her a gentle nudge with her elbow, "Abigail, who is that man?"

Abigail looked up from her plate of food and in the direction that Emma was pointing. Sitting several tables over was a young Amish man that she didn't recognize. He was tall and thin with a shock of dark hair. Looking up, his brown eyes met Abigail's before she could look back down at her plate.

"Who is he?" Emma asked again.

Abigail shrugged her shoulders, "I have no idea."

Recently, many new couples had been moving into their community with their families.

Families...the word alone made Abigail want to cry.

She would never have a family of her own.

Looking back, she should have realized that things with Jacob had never been good. In their five years together, he had never once mentioned marriage, even while all their other friends had been tying the knot. Jacob had only ever been interested in having fun. He liked to have his own way and always got what he wanted.

The realization that Abigail had simply been someone for him to use for his enjoyment was almost more than she could stand. While she had been planning her future with him, to Jacob she was simply a stepping stone to his life apart from her.

"Pete, Lovina," She heard a voice speaking to her parents, "I have someone I want you to meet."

Abigail looked up in time to see their bishop introducing her parents to the stranger Emma had pointed out.

"This is Noah Abrams," the bishop was explaining, "He's new to the community."

Noah nodded his head and stretched out his hand to take her father's, "Mr. Schroder, it's good to meet you and your family."

Abigail's father smiled and said, "It's good to have you in the community, Noah! I'd like you to meet my wife, Lovina, and our daughters, Sally, Emma, and Abigail."

Noah nodded his head to each of the girls. It seemed to Abigail that his gaze paused on her. Staring into his dark chocolate eyes was almost more than she could bear and she had to look down at her lap.

"Oh, Abigail," Sally breathed softly as the bishop led him on to speak to someone else, "Where do you suppose his wife is? Do you think he's married? It's hard to imagine that anyone that *wunderbar gut* looking would be single!"

Abigail gave her sister a solemn glance and then continued to play with her food.

It was true, the stranger was handsome. His body was so tall and fit, his dark hair so wavy, and his eyes so incredibly deep. When he had looked at her, Abigail almost felt as if Noah Abrams could look into her very soul.

"*Ach*, Abigail," she scolded herself silently, "You better stop."

Surely looking at men was not a good idea for Abigail. When Jacob had left so had all hopes of her future; it was time she accepted that truth completely. Besides, Noah Abrams was probably married.

Chapter Three

Monday morning was the start of a new week and the day that Abigail went to go help out Mandy Eicher. Mandy was the Amish community's seamstress. Each week she took on sewing and, with her youngest daughter recently married, the workload was more than Mandy could handle on her own.

Despite the beautiful spring weather, the five-minute walk to the Eicher house left Abigail feeling morose. She wondered if this was to be the rest of her life. She wondered if each day she would do the same thing until she was an old maid.

Wiping a tear from her eye, Abigail softly whispered, "Why, Lord? What kind of life am I going to lead? If this is all you have planned for me and I am never to have the dearest wishes of my heart, why did you give me life at all?"

Abigail didn't knock on Mandy's door; instead, she simply turned the knob and stepped into the backroom where Mandy worked on the sewing.

Surprisingly enough, Mandy was not at her old fashioned sewing machine yet and the pile of laundry was still lying untouched on the table.

"Hmmm," Abigail whispered to herself, "This isn't like the Mandy that I know."

"Mandy," she called out as she started to sort through a pile of dresses, "Mandy, are ya home?"

Suddenly, the form of a little girl came scampering into the sewing room, filling the area with her giggles.

"Hi!" She greeted Abigail, a huge smile stretched across her pretty round face, "What's your name?"

Abigail raised her eyebrows in surprise. While she knew that Mandy had several grandchildren, she had never met this child before.

"I'm Abigail." Despite Abigail's sad mood, something about the little girl instantly warmed her heart.

The child pushed back a blonde curl that had escaped from her prayer cap and smiled, "Well, it's good to meet you, Abigail! My name is Katie and I'm five years old."

She seemed like such a little lady that Abigail couldn't help but smile back. She wanted to pick Katie up and give her a hug.

"You're nice," Katie announced.

"Where are your parents?" Abigail asked as she foraged through her pocket and pulled out a piece of candy to offer the child.

"Ooohhh, candy!" Katie squealed as she took the piece of peppermint, "*Danki*, Abigail! My *daed* had to go work on our new house today, so I have to stay here with Aunt Mandy."

"What about your mama?"

Katie shrugged sadly, her face suddenly clouding over, "I never had one...but I want one awful badly! Daddy says that we just have to wait on God to bring us a new one, but He sure is taking a long time. I'm starting to wonder if God ever wants me to get a new *Mamm*!"

"Oh, there you are!" Mandy let out a sigh of relief as she stepped into the room, "Katie, I have been looking all over the house for you! Where have you been?"

The little girl shrugged her shoulders, "Right here, Aunt Mandy!"

Mandy shook her head and took a deep breath, "*Gut* morning, Abigail. I am so sorry to keep you waiting. It's been a long time since I've had a little child around the house." Putting her hand on Katie's head, Mandy went on to say, "She's my great-niece. Katie and her dad just moved to the community and he's working to build a house. I've agreed to let them stay here and watch her during the day until his house gets finished..." Mandy took a deep breath and let it out, "I'm really not sure what he will do with her after that."

Abigail had always respected Mandy but hearing her talk of Katie as if she was nothing more than a burden broke her heart.

Katie got down on the floor to chase after a glass marble as Mandy went on to announce, "His wife died when Katie was born. If he had any sense, he would have remarried then. As things are now, he has no one to watch Katie and no hopes of things ever getting better!"

Abigail watched the little girl and shook her head sadly. It was strange to think that she wasn't the only one whose heart had been broken by loss. She knew what it was like to love someone and then lose them.

"Do you want me to get started on sewing one of these dresses?" Abigail asked softly as she motioned toward the pile of clothes.

Mandy shook her head, "Actually, I have a better use for you today, Abigail. I'll do most of the sewing if you'll just keep up with Katie. Would you mind?"

Would she mind? Abigail could think of no better job in the world!

Chapter Four

Often, Abigail found working at Mandy's to be a bit of a drag. The piles of clothing seemed never-ending and the hours would pass so slowly. Today, however, things were different.

Keeping up with Katie was the most enjoyable job that Abigail had ever done. She played hide-n-go-seek with the little girl, they baked cookies together, and they went out to the barn to look at the calves.

As the hours of the afternoon started to fade away, Abigail took Katie inside and helped her sew a little pincushion from some leftover scraps of material.

"You are a wonder with that child," Mandy announced with a smile as she watch Katie sitting quietly on the floor playing with the pincushion she had just made, "I thought I would pull my hair out before you came today!"

"She's a treasure," Abigail replied.

She was going to say more, but suddenly the voice of men interrupted her thoughts. Mandy's husband had returned home and with him was someone else.

"Aunt Mandy, where are you?"

"Back here!"

"It's Daddy!" Katie announced as she jumped up from her place on the floor, "Daddy, Daddy, come here!"

The figure of a tall man stepped into the sewing room and Katie went running to his side, "Daddy, Daddy, pick me up! I've got something to show you!"

Noah Abrams.

Abigail knew it was him as soon as she heard his voice. Although she had only seen him for a few minutes at church, it seemed she had memorized him instantly.

"Ah, a pincushion," he was exclaiming as he looked over Katie's project, "You'll have to be careful when playing with pins!"

"That's what Abigail already told me," Katie laughed as her father tickled her chin, "She's the nice lady who helped me!"

Noah finally looked up and let his eyes meet Abigail's. With a smile of recognition, he nodded his head, "Abigail Schroder, right?"

Abigail found herself tempted to look down at the floor in sudden awkwardness, "That's right."

"Abigail saved me today, Noah," Mandy was quick to announce as she cut a piece of thread on a pair of pants and put them aside, "I was able to get so much more work done while she kept Katie entertained."

"Abigail is so much fun!" Katie said with a smile before turning to Abigail, "Abigail are you going to come back to play with me tomorrow?"

"No, I'm afraid not." Abigail almost hated to tell the little girl, "I only come help your Aunt Mandy on Mondays and Fridays."

Katie's little smile quickly turned into a frown, "But I want you to come back!"

"Katie," Noah scolded gently, "Don't be rude. Miss Abigail may have other things she needs to do. You'll see her soon. Now tell her good night and go get washed up for supper."

Katie tried to smile, but her chin quivered as she got out of her father's arms and went over to give Abigail a hug.

"Bye, Abigail," the little girl whispered, "I hope you'll come back to see me again."

Mandy led Katie out of the room to go get ready for supper, leaving Noah and Abigail alone.

They stood alone in awkward silence until Abigail finally started to gather her things.

"Well," Abigail took a deep breath, "Until Friday, I suppose."

"I didn't see a buggy when I pulled up." Noah said before Abigail could reach the door, "Do you have a driver coming?"

Abigail shook her head, "I walk home."

"Don't do that. My buggy is still hitched up. I can give you a ride back while I wait on Aunt Mandy to get supper."

Abigail wanted to protest but Noah stopped her.

"No 'buts'," he announced with a smile, "I should do something to repay you for your kindness to my little girl."

With a nod, Abigail found herself agreeing and allowed Noah Abrams to lead her out to his buggy.

Chapter Five

Abigail had not been alone with a man since Jacob left. Even though her house was just down the road, she wondered if she could bear the trip.

"I'm glad we could get a chance to talk," Noah announced as he guided his horse down the gravel drive that led to the road, "Truth be told, I'm at my wits end now that I'm here at my aunt's house. Until I get my own home finished, I have to leave Katie there and Aunt Mandy simply doesn't have the energy needed to take care of a little girl."

Abigail nodded sympathetically, "What do you plan to do?"

"Oh, things will be fine once I get my house finished and my farm up and running. I'm used to taking care of Katie. I just can't build a house with her by my side. A worksite isn't a safe place for a five-year-old."

Although Katie was a sweet child, Abigail tried to imagine how hard it would be for this poor man to try to care for her while running a farm.

"I honestly don't see how you do it all alone," Abigail announced before she could think better of her words, "It must be difficult with no wife."

Suddenly, Abigail felt her face growing warm. She wondered if her embarrassment was showing. Surely her ears must be as red as the beets that grew in her mom's garden.

"It is very rough," Noah replied with a sigh, "Even after all these years, it isn't always easy. Sometimes I doubt my ability to raise a little girl on my own but it seems to be the job that God has given me."

Abigail braved a glance at the man beside her. He looked so solemn, so completely resigned to his future. Abigail could tell that Noah Abrams had faced many difficulties in his life.

"Miss Schroder," Noah began, his voice sounding almost nervous, "I know you're too busy to even consider it, but, until I get my house finished, I need a babysitter for Katie. My aunt just can't seem to do it anymore. Would you be willing to take on the job?"

Would she?! Abigail had to fight to keep from clapping her hands in excitement. The idea of going a whole week without seeing Katie had made life seem so hollow; his job offer truly seemed like an answer to her prayers.

"Yes," She replied without any hesitation, "I can't think of anything I would love any more!"

Noah looked to Abigail and smiled. In that instant, it seemed that a weight had been lifted off his shoulders. Suddenly, he seemed carefree and happy, and whistled the rest of the way to the Schroder house.

Noah started picking Abigail up in his buggy every morning and taking her to his aunt's house where she would spend the day watching little Katie. Each day that passed, the small child became even more dear to Abigail and, surprisingly enough, so did Noah.

Abigail certainly wasn't allowing herself to entertain ideas about the handsome young widower, but she couldn't deny that a tiny shoot of hope was beginning to grow in her heart. Just like the tiny beans that had sprouted in the garden, Abigail was beginning to feel like her heart was thawing and that perhaps there was room for someone other than Jacob.

Chapter Six

Abigail had been watching little Katie daily for six weeks when Noah arrived at her house one bright Tuesday morning with a certain mischievous grin on his face. Unlike most mornings, he had small daughter at his side and a wicker basket loaded into the back of the wagon.

"*Gut* morning, Abigail!" Noah exclaimed as he reached out to help her up onto the seat, "Are you ready for a big adventure?"

Katie was grinning from ear-to-ear, leaving Abigail to wonder exactly what was up Noah Abram's sleeve.

"I don't know," Abigail replied with a laugh as she settled down on the other side of Katie, "I'm never very adventurous. What do you have planned?"

"You'll see," Noah promised with a wink.

To Abigail's surprise, Noah drove his buggy past Mandy's house and on down the road.

"Where are we going?" Katie asked, her confusion making it obvious that she was just as uncertain about the day as Abigail.

"Wait and see," Noah said as he wrapped an arm around his little child's shoulder.

Together, the three of them traveled down a small country road and turned onto a gravel driveway lined with blossoming apple trees.

"It's so beautiful!" Katie squealed as she reached out to try to touch one of the pink blossoms, "Where are we going, Daddy? This can't be the regular world, can it, Abigail?"

It certainly didn't feel like the regular world, even to Abigail. It felt like they were entering a magical land where dreams came true. Abigail took a deep breath, drawing in the scent of the wildflowers growing in the surrounding meadows. This felt like a place where she could finally release all the pain from her past and leave her worries behind.

"Look up there," Noah pointed ahead of them.

There at the end of the driveway, was a huge two-story white farmhouse.

"Oh, Daddy," Katie breathed softly, "Who owns this house?"

"We do, sweetheart!"

The house was beautiful, but it wasn't what held Abigail's attention. Instead, she found herself staring at Noah as he chatted with his daughter about their new home. It was the first time Abigail had seen him so happy. His dark brown eyes were glimmering and he was smiling like a little boy. Something about him was captivating.

Noah stopped the buggy beside the house and hopped down from his seat.

"This is it," He kept repeating as he led Katie and Abigail up onto the porch, "Sure, it's not quite finished yet. It will probably be another week before we can move in, but this is it! We have a home!"

"We have a home!" Katie repeated as she jumped up and down, clapping her hands together, "Did you hear that Abigail, we have a home!"

Abigail didn't even find herself shying away or correcting the little girl's mistake; the moment was simply too precious and Abigail discovered that she truly wished that this was her home as well.

They spend the day touring the large house and looking over the property. Noah had purchased two-hundred acres and explained his plans to build various barns to hold different animals along with his hopes to plant different kinds of grain.

Each moment that passed, Abigail found herself falling a little more in love with the man before her.

Certainly, Noah was not Jacob, but he was so much more. Selfless, caring, and gentle, Abigail wished that she had been able to meet Noah first.

Chapter Seven

Noah finished the afternoon off with a picnic by the side of the creek that trickled through his property. He had packed a delicious lunch of fried chicken, mashed potatoes, and strawberries.

"Daddy," Katie jumped up as soon as she had finished her last bite, "Can I go play in the water?"

Noah nodded, "Of course!"

Katie giggled with excitement as she hurried down to the bubbling water.

"Is she safe by herself?" Abigail asked, wondering if she should go along.

Noah nodded, "We can see her from here and the creek is only an inch deep."

Of course, Noah knew everything about the safety of the property. Abigail let out a sigh of relief as she leaned back on her elbows. She just wanted to sit peacefully and soak in the day. She wished that this afternoon never had to end.

"This is the prettiest place I've ever seen," Abigail commented.

Noah smiled, "I've always dreamed of living on a farm like this. Back in Ohio, I had a nice place, but it was just functional. I want Katie to grow up on a farm like this. It was what Lizzy wanted too..." Suddenly, his voice trailed off and his happy smile was totally replaced by something much more sober.

"Was Lizzy your wife?" Abigail ventured to ask, wondering if she should even tackle a subject that obviously brought him so much pain.

Noah nodded his head and started absentmindedly pulling pieces of grass out of the ground, "Lizzy and I got together when we were sixteen years old, and got married before we turned twenty. She was a good girl, Abigail. She had my whole heart in a way I never thought anyone else ever could..."

"What happened?"

Noah's gaze turned to the creek where his little girl was playing, "Katie happened. We wanted a baby so much, but it seems that Lizzy wasn't strong enough to handle a pregnancy. There were so many complications. When Katie was born, there was trouble and she had to go stay in the hospital. She only lived for one night." Noah shook his head, "I promised her so many things, Abigail. Promises that, sometimes, I'm not sure that I can keep. Sometimes I'm so scared that I'm going to fail her."

Noah reached up and brushed a tear away from his cheek. Watching his pain made Abigail's heart ache.

"Noah," she said in little more than a whisper, "I think you're doing everything right."

Noah turned to look at her. His eyes were red from fighting back his tears.

"*Ach*, Abigail," he muttered, "You know exactly how to help me."

In an unexpected turn of events, he reached out and gently cradled Abigail's face in his large hand.

"Daddy!" Katie's voice interrupted them, and Noah quickly withdrew.

"Daddy, Abigail, look!" Katie squealed as she came running toward their picnic spot, "I caught a fish!"

She held out her fist and revealed a tiny minnow that she had caught in the creek, "Can we cook him for supper?"

Noah and Abigail looked at each other and burst into laughter. Their special moment was over, but Abigail felt as if something between them had certainly changed forever.

Chapter Eight

Before taking her home, Noah stopped by Mandy's house.

"I'm going to take Katie in so she can go on and get ready for bed," he explained as he helped the little girl down from the buggy.

"I'll go in and say hello to your aunt," Abigail said as she took his hand in hers to get down from her seat.

Noah took Katie back into her bedroom to get changed for bed and Abigail started toward the sewing room.

As she neared the sewing room door, she could hear Mandy's voice, "Noah's almost done with his house," she was saying, "I'll be so glad once he moves out!"

Abigail lifted her hand to knock against the door, but stopped when she heard another voice speak up, "Have you seen the way that Abigail throws herself at your nephew?"

"*Ach*, yes," Abigail could see Mandy shaking her head sadly through a crack in the door, "I'm afraid that the poor girl is simply in for even more heartbreak. After being jilted by Jacob back in the spring, she must be so desperate!"

"So you don't think Noah has any interest in her?"

Mandy let out a disgusted laugh, "Most certainly not! He's used her as a babysitter, but he's had women help him out before. My sister said one girl in Ohio was almost certain that he would propose...as soon as he heard the rumors, he let her go."

Rachel Miller was clucking her tongue in condescending sadness.

"I wish he would, but Noah will never marry. He made a promise to his wife and that's final. I just wish he'd stop leading these poor girls to believe there is hope!" Mandy continued on, but Abigail couldn't bear to listen anymore. Instead, she turned and silently hurried out the side door, unwilling to wait for Noah to take her home.

Abigail couldn't stop the flood of tears that kept running down her cheeks. She wondered if she could even make it back to her house before she completely fell apart.

She could hear footsteps behind her, their sound only making it worse as she realized that she was being followed.

"Abigail," Noah called out as he ran up behind her, "Abigail, what's wrong?"

"Nothing!" Abigail exclaimed bitterly as she wrapped her arms across her chest, "I feel sick. I've got to get home."

With longer legs, Noah quickly overtook her.

"Abigail," he exclaimed as stood in front of her to block her way, "Can't I at least take you home? You've been crying! Why are you so upset? What has happened?"

"Nothing!" Abigail insisted as she stomped her foot against the ground, "Just let me go!"

When Noah saw that there was nothing he could do to stop her, he stepped out of the way and let Abigail pass.

How could I have been so foolish? Abigail asked herself as she marched down the road toward her house, *I should have never trusted another man! I should have never trusted God to have a plan for me!*

The next morning, Abigail stayed home from work. When Noah came to pick her up, she had her sister Sally go with him instead.

Chapter Nine

Each minute of the day had been agony. She had missed Katie, and she had missed Noah. How she had come to look forward to their time together! Abigail already found herself missing Noah much more than she had ever missed Jacob.

Abigail was out in the chicken house gathering eggs and trying not to cry when she heard a buggy pull into their yard.

Stepping out to check on who might be visiting, she was surprised to see Noah's buggy. On the seat beside him were Sally and Katie.

"Why are they home so early?" Abigail wondered to herself. She had planned to hide away inside the house when they returned, making it impossible to be faced with seeing him. Now she had no way to escape.

Noah scanned the yard as he helped both her sister and Katie down from the buggy.

"Where is Abigail?" She could hear the little girl ask.

"I don't know," Sally replied, "But you can come inside and we'll look for her. I'll also give you a piece of chocolate cake!"

Noah's eyes were scanning the property. When he turned to look her way, Abigail grabbed for the chicken house door, ready to hide wherever she could; however, she wasn't fast enough. In an instant, Noah's eyes were locked on her.

"Abigail, wait!" He exclaimed, making large strides in her direction, "We have to talk!"

"There's nothing to talk about."

Noah was now by her side.

"Abigail," Noah took a deep breath and caught her hand in his, "What's wrong? I thought that you were having a good time taking care of little Katie. Why would you want to quit now?"

"You don't understand, do you?" Abigail shook her head sadly, "I can't do it anymore, Noah! I just can't!"

"Why? If it's because of what happened on the picnic, I am truly sorry. I acted out of hast and I shouldn't have. I should never have touched you..."

Abigail shook her head. She couldn't let Noah think that she was rejecting him.

"No, no, no!" She exclaimed, closing her eyes and trying to keep the tears from pouring like rain, "It's not that at all. Oh, Noah, you don't understand. I overheard your aunt talking. She said that you will never get married again, that your wife made you promise that you wouldn't! I can't stand to lose you, Noah, I just can't! I love you far too much for that. If we can't ever be together, than I can't be around you at all!"

Noah let out something that sounded almost like a sigh of relief, "Abigail, dear Abigail," he reached up and gently brushed away her tears with the tip of his finger, "I thought that you hated me. You poor, dear girl! My aunt knows some things, but she doesn't know everything. When Lizzy died, she did make me promise things. She made me promise that I would take care of Katie, that I would love her, that I would do what was best for her, that I would give her a good home...and then she made me promise that I would not marry again until I found someone who I truly love, someone who will take good care of our little girl and who will take good care of me. Abigail, I have avoided women for that very reason. I have never felt like God had put the right one in my path. I never felt like any woman I met would ever be able to fill the void that Lizzy left in my heart."

His words...they almost gave her hope. Abigail took a deep breath and shook her head, "Noah, I know you can never feel that way about me."

Noah put his hands on her shoulders and stared into her eyes, "Abigail, you don't know how special you've become to me."

Suddenly, the words broke something deep inside of Abigail. It felt like the wall she had built around her heart was suddenly shattered into a million pieces as she realized that she truly did have hope.

"It can be hard to explain what is in my heart," Noah whispered as he leaned his forehead against hers, "But you need to know that what is in my heart is you, Abigail Schroder."

"Oh Noah," she whispered the words softly against his lips, "You are my whole heart as well."

Suddenly, their lips met in love's first kiss. As Noah pulled her closer against his strong body, Abigail could feel her broken heart begin to heal. Just when she thought that God had given up on her future, He had continued to work out His plans in her life. When Abigail had been ready to give up on ever having her own family, God had brought this wonderful *gut* man to her side.

Once their kiss was over, Abigail found herself leaning her head against this dear man's shoulder.

"Noah," she whispered gently, "Oh, Noah, I do love you so."

Suddenly, the sound of childish laughter brought them back to reality as Katie emerged from the large farmhouse and started bouncing across the yard.

"Daddy," Katie squealed as she ran to him and wrapped her arms around his legs, "Does this mean I'm going to get a new *Mamm*?"

Noah looked at Abigail and winked.

"It just might," he told her as he scooped the little girl up into his arms, "We will just have to ask her." Turning to look at Abigail, Noah asked, "Miss Schroder, would you do us the honor of being Katie's new *Mamm*? And my new wife?"

Abigail could hardly speak over the pounding of her joyful heart, "Nothing would make me any happier!"

She reached out and wrapped her arms around both Noah and Katie, pulling her new family close against her.

God truly had a plan after all.

BENEATH THE AMISH SKY

NIKKI SALEM

Chapter One

She didn't love him.

She'd never love him.

Anna knew better than to think in absolutes, knew that she shouldn't assume she knew better than her father, but she would never love Samuel. Not if she was given a thousand years, not if he were actually closer to her age.

She was hardly twenty-one.

Hardly out of age for going to Sings and getting to court properly, her Rumspringa wasn't even finished.

Her father thought he knew what was best for her.

Samuel was an absolute nightmare though.

He was almost thirty-five, married once but his wife left to be English.

When Anna had first heard about this she felt terrible for him. It was horrifying to think that someone you pledged your life to could just leave you behind without a second thought. To live a life neither of you were familiar with. Anna couldn't imagine how selfish and cruel his ex-wife must have been. Leaving behind a chance at growing a family, at starting a life together, sounded outrageous-

Until she properly got to know Samuel.

His wife had made the right decision, and as she knew him better Anna began to envy the mystery woman who had flown the coup.

Samuel was boring, uninteresting, repetitive. He worked in the church, which her father found more than respectable, and so all he spoke of was the church. He went on for literal hours about repairs he wanted to do to the meeting building, hardly pausing to breathe. He didn't care to listen to her, or to stop once she was obviously uncomfortable. In all of the hours her parents had let him speak with her, she'd probably spoken less than twenty words.

She didn't want to have to live with that forever.

Anna couldn't imagine another sixty years, or more, of her life dedicated to this man who didn't care about anything but himself and the image the church gave him.

She couldn't see herself ever loving him, so marriage was a horrifying prospect.

The evening sun was just beginning to settle on the edge of the horizon. Her father had made up his mind, and all she could do was hope to dissuade him somehow. Gathering the last of the laundry for the next day, she listened for his tell-tale footsteps.

He was her father, she knew it was sad to be so nervous, but she was.

Sucking in a deep breath, she urged her feet forward, out to the kitchen where he was standing and drinking water.

"Father, may we speak?" she asked, her hands settled in front of her.

"Yes, what is it?" he asked, he was covered in mud from the day's work.

"I can't marry Samuel," she laid the words out neatly between them. Her father's mood seemed to immediately crumple into aggravation.

"You will," he replied back simply.

"Father I don't love him," she said, shaking her head. "He's so boring, I can't imagine a worse match," she admitted, approaching him.

"What does that matter?" her father asked, his voice raising. "You're supposed to be building a home and a family together, you'll love him in the end," he shook his head.

"I won't marry him," she said, standing her ground in a way she never had with her father.

"Are you saying my decisions aren't good enough for you?" he asked, slamming his hat down on the table.

"No, I-"

"You are my daughter, you had your chance to choose, that's over," he said sternly.

"I can still choose to leave," she said, hoping the words would bite him so he'd realize what he was saying. His face dropped into one of dark anger.

"If you will not listen to me, you *can* leave," his voice was like the grave, and it stung her.

"Father-"

"I will not have you speaking out against me, I make the decisions, I would rather have you married with him than unmarried with nothing but a dream of romance," her father was red faced in anger.

"Then I'll leave!" she shot back, the words slipped past her lips before she could catch them.

The air between them was still and quiet.

The moment stretched thinly, until a cough in the next room let Anna know her mother was nearby. She had a habit of listening in on conversations, and Anna couldn't hold it against her.

"I'll be gone by tomorrow night," Anna added, the words terrifying and unreal feeling even as she said them.

***

She didn't sleep that night.

Anna spent the night shoving what she could into a couple bags. Her clothing was plain, but plenty. She wasn't sure what she was planning on doing, on where she was planning on going. She just knew that if she spent another night under the same roof as her father she was going to explode.

Samuel wasn't an option.

In the blue light of morning she heard her father leave for his work.

Out her window she watched him pause for a moment, looking towards her window, and then step up onto his buggy and leave.

Just as well, she reminded herself, it would be easier to leave if he wasn't there.

As she started to drag her two bags to the front, her mother stopped her.

"Anna," her mother said, soothing a hand over Anna's right arm. "Are you sure you want to do this?" she asked softly.

"No," Anna admitted. "The only thing I'm sure I want in this world is that I do not want to be with Samuel," she explained.

"You could stay, reason with him, be patient with your father," her mother said gently.

"You know better than I do that's not an option," Anna sighed. "It's easier this way, otherwise I know I'd end up marrying Samuel," she explained.

"Alright," her mother replied. "You should take this though," she added, handing a small envelope to Anna. "It'll get you through long enough until you get a job," she tucked her arms tight around Anna. "You can always come back to me, my Anna, your father is stubborn but he'll miss you," she explained.

"He'll not want me back after this," Anna argued, feeling tears prickle at her eyes.

"You're his daughter, he always will have a spot for you," she countered,

"Thank you, mother," Anna sobbed, rubbing her eyes as the tears free fell.

"Of course my daughter," her mother answered, hugging her again. "I love you very much, I'll do anything for you to be happy," she added.

When her mother set to starting to clean laundry for the day, Anna was forced to start her journey.

The world looked too ordinary, too regular, for what day it was.

She steeled herself, and started her walk out of the village she'd always lived in. Out to where she knew cars would take her to a city, to a place so impossibly different and strange to her.

Anything was better than Samuel, though.

Chapter Two

Within her first week she'd already gone through over half of the three thousand her mother left her.

Anna was an intelligent girl, though. She'd found a room to rent in a Victorian home, something not too unfamiliar from what homes she was used to, for just a couple hundred a month. She paid six months of it in advance, and spent the rest on clothes, food, and a phone, to make herself to fit in.

Her new landlady, Holly, was to thank for most of the ideas and shopping.

She was a forty year old woman, and so kind, Anna was thankful she'd found her listing in the news paper. Not everything was as unfamiliar as she'd imagined.

People treated her differently, but as long as she ignored them they'd have nothing to say.

A couple men had talked to her, shown interest in her, but she had ignored all of them. She was sure she was being rude, she was sure that she'd never make any friends this way, but she also was sure that friendship wasn't what these men were wanting.

She'd never date.

Never go after any men, or marry.

She'd decided this on the ride out from her home.

Anna knew that she'd never find a man, an English man, who her parents would approve of. She couldn't marry someone they didn't approve of, even if she wasn't a part of the church anymore. In her heart she knew it would be the wrong thing to do.

She loved the idea of love, of finding someone who you match with perfectly, but she couldn't feel right being in that kind of love if it meant her family would look down on her for it.

She already had enough shame to bear.

The only thing left to do was to find a job.

Holly had gathered a list of places for Anna to look. Everything ranging from lawyer's offices, to factories that made holiday chocolate all year round.

She'd bought comfortable shoes, though, and she was happy to go to each business and try to impress with what she could. There wasn't much on her resume, but she had to try.

If not she'd have squandered her mother's money for nothing.

The general response to her from most companies was an extreme naked curiosity. They'd look at her like she grew a few extra heads during the conversation, and keep her there to talk to them for a bit. Just when she'd think she was closing the deal on the job, most places would apologize and say they were looking for someone with more experience.

She took that to mean they wanted someone who could operate a computer.

Her courage was waning, she wanted to get hired quickly, to be able to send her mother back a return of what she'd been given. Nothing was turning up, though, after a week and a half of, almost constant, searching.

Fearful for what was leftover of the money, not wanting to let herself have too much access to it, Anna found herself inside a bank.

The building was cold, refreshing against the summer sun, and empty besides her and a teller behind one of the long counters.

He caught her eyes, and a curdling guild set low in her stomach immediately.

He was gorgeous.

This stranger, with a name tag that shimmered out Andre, held her attention with more strength than Samuel had in any of the time she'd known him. His curly brown hair was combed back away from strong cheekbones and glittering green eyes. His shoulders looked broad, strong, and he seemed taller than most men she'd seen in the city.

When he looked up back at her, Anna felt chills run through her, and her face heated.

She didn't need to think about that, though, she was on a mission.

"Good afternoon," he greeted, setting aside the papers he was looking at. His voice was deep, echoing in the empty bank.

"Good afternoon," she mirrored. "I was hoping to open an account," she said, unsure how to phrase this. She regretted not asking Holly for help on this.

"I can help you with that," he smiled, turning to his computer. "Checking or savings?" he asked, typing.

"Checking, please," she responded, letting her eyes fall on his hands for just a moment before she looked away.

"Do you have two kinds of identification?" he asked, his typing stopped.

"Yes," she answered, pulling out the state ID she'd gotten just in the last week, and her birth certificate.

He accepted them and then froze.

"Are you Amish?" he asked, he looked stunned. "Or- were- you Amish?" he corrected himself, something nobody else had done.

"I was," she agreed. Her birth certificate named the only Amish town within a hundred miles.

"I was as well," he said, his eyes shining with nostalgia.

"You were?" she said, surprised for once.

"Yes, I was with a town in Idaho, I've been out of the church for five years," he answered.

"I just left the church almost two weeks ago," Anna said meekly.

"Well, welcome to the madness," he replied, a joke in his voice. She immediately felt comfortable with him.

This had never happened to her before.

"Thank you," she answered, unsure of the proper reply.

"I'll go ahead and set up your account," he started typing her information into the computer. "Will you want to use direct deposit for your job?" he asked, handing back her documents.

"I don't have a job yet," she admitted, embarrassed.

He typed something, and then paused for a moment.

"Have you applied here?" he asked.

"No," she answered, embarrassed at herself for overlooking the opportunity.

"We've been holding walk-in interviews, I can get the manager over to talk with you, if you'd like," he offered. "They're very happy to train, here," he said.

"That would be amazing," Anna said, surprised at her own luck.

As she watched him walk away, she could feel herself getting quickly attached. She knew she'd promised herself she'd stay away from boys.

She'd sworn she wouldn't date.

Still, she felt an attraction, an interest in him, that she'd never felt with anyone else. If she was going to live an English life, she owed herself to at least properly try it.

***

The interview was simple.

An older man, older than her father, asked her a handful of questions about her life an experience. He didn't seem phased that she'd never touched a computer until the last couple of weeks.

She stood up as the interview ended, expecting him to say they were looking for someone with more experience.

"Would you be available to start training tomorrow?" he asked instead, opening the door into for her.

"Yes!"

Chapter Three

Working with Andre was testing her convictions.

He was placed in charge of training her, helping her figure out the computers and the cash counting machines. Andre was patient, kind, and took his time with her even when customers were around.

She learned he'd moved into the state right after he left the church. He didn't own a television, but watched shows on a computer he had a home. She learned he liked to order lunch in, but always forgot to eat breakfast.

She learned he was incredibly generous with his smiles.

Regardless of how simple, how quick, her attachment to him had been within the first couple minutes of meeting him, it had grown into something stronger.

They bonded over talking about similar life experiences, over finding out what differences set them apart. He'd ridden in cars a lot growing up, none owned by his family, while she'd never been in a computer until the last couple weeks.

He was like a piece of her home that she'd left behind.

A warm blanket in the starkness of the new world she was getting used to.

A couple weeks into working together he asked her to dinner, and she couldn't make herself say no.

He picked a place close to her home, and she was both thrilled and terrified.

Holly immediately took the helm.

"I haven't dated in ten years, but you make me feel like I'm the one going out to night," Holly laughed, helping her pick out something to wear. "It's so funny that you're both Amish, isn't it?" she asked, Anna couldn't see the humor, but she nodded anyways.

"I think blue is really the best color for you," Holly said, pulling back Anna's hair so that it didn't cover the simple dress too much.

"Thank you," Anna said.

"But- are you sure you don't want to wear something brighter? Something turquoise and bright would really catch his eye," Holly offered, looking her over.

"No, for him I'd prefer to be myself," Anna smiled.

"Mm, alright," Holly tapped her shoulder, and Anna leaned her head back to let her braid her hair. They'd grown close very quickly, and Anna was glad to have someone in her corner. "He may be Amish, but he's still a boy, if you need anything please call me," Holly said, pausing to look Anna over in the mirror again. "You're gonna knock his socks off," she added, smiling.

***

The restaurant was busy when Anna arrived. She was early, so she requested a table, and then sat there and stared at the crowd.

She couldn't imagine what kinds of lives everyone in that building led. Jobs she'd probably never heard of, homes and cars that would blow her mind, problems she couldn't fathom. She couldn't imagine growing up in a world like this.

Anna listened to small snippets of conversations, catching foreign sounding ideas and words, until Andre arrived.

She was the one blown away.

He looked like he'd stepped out of a magazine. She was suddenly stunned to remember that he'd started out like her.

He'd integrated so well into this world that nobody around them would ever guess that he was Amish.

With her, she was sure people would figure it out.

He was amazing.

"Sorry I'm a little late, my Uber got lost," he apologized, sitting across from her.

"It's fine," she shook her head, smiling. She wasn't quite sure what an Uber was, but she told herself she'd ask him later.

The beginning of the date was jittery, she was nervous, and he seemed to be able to tell. She wanted to make a good impression, but was terrified that trying too hard would make her look like she'd forgotten her parents and church.

By the time they finished eating, though, she'd calmed down.

"Why did you leave the church, if I can ask," he said, stacking their plates he slid them to the end of the table.

"Oh, um," Anna wasn't sure how to explain it. She couldn't say she refused marriage, it would look like she'd never wanted to date anyone ever, but she knew she really wanted to date Andre. "My father and I had a disagreement, and he told me to leave," she explained, feeling shame at the explanation.

"Oh, I'm sorry," he said sincerely.

"It's fine," she lied. "I'm enjoying seeing what life out here is like," she admitted.

"I'm glad you're having a good time," he smiled. "So you'd rather be out here?" he asked.

"I'm not sure about that," she shook her head. "I just couldn't stay there," she tried to explain.

"Ah, I completely understand that," he agreed, take one last sip of his water.

"What about you? Why are you out here?" she asked.

"Mm, same thing, disagreements," he said. Anna wondered, her heart in her stomach, if he'd had a similar experience to her. She tried to picture him being forced into marriage, and the idea made her ache for him.

She was glad that his experiences led to him being in front of her, but was upset that it meant he had to be away from his family and the church.

"I want to go back, though," he admitted.

"Really?" Anna was surprised.

"Yes, of course, maybe not the same town, or the same people, but I miss the church. There's no sense of community or wholeness out here, I miss that so much it hurts," he explained.

"Oh," she said, surprised by him again.

She hadn't considered going back.

She'd only been gone a couple of weeks, and although she missed her family and connections she still felt better out in the world than stuck being married to Samuel. If he wanted to go back then her flirting with him was pointless. She wouldn't return with him and risk her father being disappointed in her.

Anna confirmed with herself that she was better off when she had sworn off dating.

When she finally decided this, looking back up at Andre he seemed concerned.

"What's wrong?" he asked, setting down his drink.

"Oh, nothing, I was just thinking about home," she lied.

"I get that," he nodded, continuing to eat.

She's have to stop seeing him.

Have to stop talking to him outside of professionally.

If he fell for her she'd end up hurting him and disappointing her family.

Anna continued to eat as she berated herself. If she was more thoughtful, more intelligent, she would have saved everyone a lot of heartache.

She'd tasted human interaction and became a glutton for it.

Chapter Four

It was harder to ignore Andre than she thought.

First of all, they worked together on every shift- which meant that he'd be within ten feet of her for most of an eight hour shift. Within the first half hour of their first shift together the following Monday he seemed to notice something had changed.

At first he spared her the embarrassment of asking her why.

They worked silently together, he helped her if she needed it, but kept his tone formal and plain. She did the same even though it hurt.

She wasn't sure why it hurt so much.

Anna hadn't known him for even a month, but looking at him and knowing she couldn't talk to him comfortably- knowing she couldn't hold his eye contact- anymore hurt her.

The first week of working together like this was like torture for her. He was a cold drink that her parched throat could never have. Their boss told them that their productivity was up and they had been doing a great job, and it was almost embarrassing. Had she been so distracted that she didn't work her best when she was talking to him?

Had she let him steal away her mind that much?

Anna was sure that the worst had passed. She was sure that he'd let go of his feelings for her, and she of hers, and that they could move on as regular coworkers. It wasn't something she was sure she wanted, and it hurt, but she told herself that it was for the best.

On the next Monday when she went in, someone was in Andre's spot besides him.

It was Kat, from the weekend, and some evening, shifts.

"Where's Andre?" Anna asked, trying to keep herself from seeming invested in the answer.

"He's out sick," Kat said, filling her drawer for the morning rush. "He called in last night," she added.

Anna's heart ached.

"What's wrong with him?" she asked.

"A flu probably," Kat guessed, shrugging. "Can you get me a couple more pens for my station before you get back here?" she asked.

"Yes, of course," Anna said, walking to the storage area.

He was sick.

He was sick and she didn't know? Her own stomach was turning and aching in fear. If she was over him why did it scare her so much just to hear he had the flu?

Why would she care so deeply?

Anna grabbed the pens and headed out.

She'd visit him after her shift.

***

Anna shouldn't have been able to get his home address.

She could have called him ahead and asked for it, but instead she asked Kat for help. If she called him her resolve would break. Anna just wanted to bring him some food and make sure he was okay. She wasn't going to stay long, she wasn't going to let herself say more than twenty words.

That's all.

She stood in front of his apartment complex, staring down the front of it like she was looking for answers.

Why did she care so much?

Why was a bag of hot soup and bread in her hand, why was she standing in front of a random man's home instead at her own home eating her own dinner? Why did it matter if he was okay?

At first she tried to convince herself that it was because he was Amish too, and that she was seeking that familial connection the entire Amish community shares. She knew that wasn't true. She knew better than to lie to herself.

Anna buzzed his room's number from the dial pad, and waited patiently.

"Hello?" he sounded sleepy and her heart warmed.

"I heard you were sick, I've brought food," eight words, she counted as she spoke them.

"I'll be right down," his voice chirped out quickly, like he was surprised. Anna was relieved he hadn't asked her to come up to him instead, she didn't want to appear to be straying any further from her convictions than she had.

"Hey," he said, opening the door after a minute. He looked ruffled, his hair askew and his shirt wrinkled. Her heart warmed at the sight of him, even when he was sick he was still handsome.

"Hi," nine words. She begged for her voice not to betray her.

"Come in, just to the lobby," he said gently, opening the door further. Anna knew she shouldn't but she did anyways.

"How are you feeling?" thirteen words. She could only allow herself seven more. If she went any further she didn't trust herself.

"A lot better," he said, fixing his hair with his hands. "I slept it off most of the day, drank a lot of tea and had a hot bath," he explained. "I should be back at work tomorrow," he added.

"That's good to hear," three words left.

"Yeah," he answered. Then paused for a moment and looked her seriously in the eyes. Anna felt like he was staring right into her mind. "How are you? You've been- different- this last week," he said. Anna considered her words carefully.

"I've been fine," she answered.

Twenty.

She needed to keep her mouth shut.

"Okay," he said gently. A silence hung between them, she knew he expected her to say more, she willed her mouth shut.

Anna handed him the bag of food, and then stepped back towards the door.

"Bye, then," he said, unsure.

Anna nodded, her hand on the handle to open it.

"Anna-" he said gently. She froze, not sure what to do. "Have I done something wrong? Have I hurt you in some way? If so, I'm sorry, I'll ask to be transferred to another location," he offered. "I've really enjoyed getting to know you, I'm sorry f I've made you unhappy," he continued.

Anna's hand tightened on the handle of the door as she felt her resolve start to unravel. He started to step away, and any less will power she had completely dissolved into the air.

"I can't go back and live there," she said softly, feeling tears prickle at her eyes. "I was foolish and got into a fight with my father, I refused to marry someone they wanted me to, and I ran off like a child," she explained, actually crying now. "You want to go back, and I can't give you that, I can't," she explained, shaking. "If I go back there my father won't care, he'll make me marry this stranger," she explained.

"Have you talked to him since then?" Andre asked, walking back to her. "It sounds like you both jumped into it quickly, have you talked about it?"

"I've only sent letters to my mother," Anna shook her head.

"I'm not even sure your town would accept me," Andre said gently. "What?"

"Come sit down," he motioned to a couple chairs in the lobby. Anna nodded and wiped the tears from her eyes. She never thought she'd like him this much.

Never even considered it.

"I was forced to leave because my village was convinced that I stole something from a brother of mine, even though I was out of town when it happened," he explained. "He told them I stole and sold one of their horses to the English, and they believed him. I was made to leave within a week," he explained.

"You wouldn't do that," she gasped, disgusted someone would spread a story like that.

"No, I wouldn't," he agreed. "My brother was always greed, though, and my father just recently passed. Their house was to be mine, and now it's his," he said.

"That's awful," Anna shook her head, upset.

"It's how it is," Andre shrugged. "I won't make you go anywhere you don't want to, I won't make you do anything you don't want to, but please don't shut me out like that anymore," he said gently.

"Okay," Anna nodded, feeling drained and embarrassed.

He was too kind, too understanding.

"I want to speak to my father," she admitted.

"Want me to be there for it?" he offered.

"Maybe," she sighed, wiping the last of the moisture off her face. "You should eat," she added.

"Alright," he stood slowly, walking her to the door. "Thank you for talking to me."

"Of course," she said, feeling foolish for treating him how she did.

Andre leaned down and kissed her forehead gently, before opening the door for her. Anna could feel her heart rushing the whole walk home.

What did she want?

Chapter Five

She was in front of her home again.

Regardless of where she went, who she was in the world, this place would always be her home.

She'd waited the entire week, had pressured herself into patience as she tried to figure out what to say. She wasn't asking to marry Andre, he hadn't asked her, but she wanted to court him.

She wanted her parents to be a part of her life.

She couldn't silence how she felt about them, she couldn't hide what her mind was doing.

She just wanted them to know how she felt.

Anna plucked up her courage and knocked on the door for the first time in her life. Before this she'd always been able to just go in. Before now this was always where she lived.

It was evening, the sun starting to drip down onto the horizon as the air cooled. Long blue shadows painted the fields and homes, and in the glow she felt nostalgic. There were footsteps inside, and she waited patiently, her heart hammering in her ears.

"Anna?" her mother gasped as she opened the door. Anna was swept into her arms, pulled tight and close, and Anna could feel the shudder of her mother starting to cry. "I thought all I'd ever see of you anymore was letters," her mother sobbed out, clutching her against herself.

"No, no, I'm here," Anna answered, hugging her back. She could feel tears pricking against her own eyes. "I need to speak to father," Anna said gently.

"He has hardly spoken since you left," her mother admitted wearily.

"Then I just need him to listen," Anna replied. She felt like she'd aged years since she had been there last, even though it had been less than two months.

"Alright," her mother nodded, patting her arm and pulling Anna into the home.

The house smelled of dinner and dishes, her mother had been cleaning when Anna arrived, and it took all of her willpower not to distract herself into helping clean.

"Anna is here," her mother said as they entered the sitting room. Her father was there, the bible in his lap. When he looked up at her, his eyes seemed so sad. Her heart broke for him.

"Father," Anna said gently, moving to sit next to him on the couch. He watched her quietly, only breaking his silence to itch his beard. She could remember growing up and pulling on his beard as a young girl. He looked so old now. "I'd like to talk to you for a short while," she explained. He nodded, and glanced up at her mother, who then went back to the kitchen to continue cleaning.

"You're not wearing English clothing," he noted.

"I'm not English," she reminded him. It was good to hear his voice. "I want to apologize for going wild as I did, and not listening to you," she explained. "I don't regret not marrying Samuel, but I do regret arguing with you and disrespecting you." He was quiet as she spoke, listening to each word she said with immense consideration.

"I have met an Amish man while I've been out there, and I wish to court him," she explained simply. "I'm not here to beg you to accept him, or to tell you that I wish to marry him, I just don't want to keep any part of my life from you," she said. Her father nodded.

"Who is this man?" he asked, his voice was patient, not accusing.

"He's a coworker of mine at a bank, he's kinda and intelligent," she answered.

"He's Amish?"

"Yes, and he wants to join the church again and it will have him," she said. "I want to come home father, he wants to come with me, I miss my family and world," she explained.

Her father was quiet for a while, mulling over everything he just heard. Anna was patient and watched him carefully. Her mother walked by the outside of the room more often than was necessary, she knew she was listening for an answer as well.

Her father took her hand gently and stared down at it.

"Your mother has missed you," he said softly. She knew that he meant he did as well, she didn't question it. "When I chased you away like I did I was brash, I wasn't thinking about what was best for everyone," he explained. "I wanted you to have marriage, to have happiness, like your mother and I have found. I didn't consider that Samuel would ever make you unhappy," he continued. "I'll meet this man," he explained.

Anna reached forward and grasped her father into her arms. She hadn't hugged him in years, hadn't thought to, but she needed to hold her father. His arms wrapped around her as well, and she felt like a child again.

"I just want you to be happy," he said, his voice went weak for a moment, and she willed herself to ignore it. If her father cried, she's save him the embarrassment of knowing she'd seen it.

"I'm sorry I didn't treat you with the respect you've earned," she responded, holding him tight.

They sat there for a moment, reunited and feeling every inch of how apart they were.

"When can I meet him?" her father asked, leaning back away from her. There was a shine to her eyes that she felt her heart warm to.

"He's outside. He dressed in clothes he still had from his last town, he's waiting just outside of the fence," she admitted, bowing her head. "He requested to meet you both," she added. Her mother now stopped in the hall, no longer pretending she was carrying laundry back and forth for the tenth time. Setting down the basket, she approached the two of them and sat her hands on her husbands shoulder.

"We'll see him," her father said, nodding.

Anna nodded, and rushed out to get him.

"They want to see you," she said gently, pulling him out of his thoughts. Anxious nerves and excitement both crossed Andre's face, and she ached to wipe the lines of stress away.

"My father has forgiven me, we're okay now," she added, trying to soothe him.

"Alright," he said, taking her hand. "I love you," he added, the crickets around them were humming to life as the sun began to really set.

"I love you too," she breathed out, amazed that the words were hers, that she really meant them.

She couldn't fear anything, nothing was scary anymore.

She was in love, and her parents accepted it.

As she led him back to the house, her hand brushing against his, glad to finally be back home.

AMISH SWEETHEARTS

ERICA FANNING

Isaac Yoder couldn't remember a time in his life when he felt so alive. It wasn't his first Sunday night out with the other Amish teenagers. In fact, he was coming up on his 18th birthday, but this night was different. There was singing and Bible reading, as well as fellowship with the young women to find a potential mate, but this time was different. His best friend since 3rd grade, Miriam Hershberger, was there for the first time. She had just turned 16. He had liked some of the other young women well enough, but when Isaac saw Miriam that night, with the twilight coming in through the church windows and the candlelight dancing off of her loose golden locks that never really stayed in her head covering, he suddenly had different feelings for her. He might have imagined it, but he was sure she had looked his way a few times that night, and it was more than just a friendly look.

His friend Joshua noticed it too. "Look at Miriam over there. She looks beautiful." He had leaned closer so that no one else could overhear. Isaac nodded. "I know how much you like her." Isaac scoffed lightly. Joshua slapped him hard enough on the back to take his breath away. "Go talk to her!"

Joshua Hostetler was Isaac's best guy friend. Isaac, Miriam, and Joshua were nearly inseparable. Even though Miriam was two years younger, she always presented herself as the oldest of the three. Even in schoolwork, Miriam could have been two grades ahead, but her father wouldn't allow it.

Miriam's father, Jacob Hershberger, was absolutely opposed to Isaac courting Miriam. Had Isaac asked yet? No, but the men in the fields talked. Many times Isaac was sure they thought he couldn't hear them, but he heard every word: Jacob desired for his eldest daughter to marry none other than Isaac's friend, Joshua. Her father was insistent that he knew what was best for his daughter. Jacob only allowed Miriam to come to the Sunday singing because she had incessantly begged him to let her be a part of the youth group since her two best friends had both been there for two years. Rumor was that Joshua had already started dating Miriam, but when Isaac asked him about it, he denied it. Tonight was proving that more than any words.

The Amish (who call themselves Plain) have what they call *Rumspringa,* or more literally, "running around." It's a time for youths ages 16-22 to find a suitable spouse. There is a common misconception that it is also a time for Plain youths to experiment with the English (non-Plain) world. Though they have the option to do so, *Rumspringa* is more for finding a spouse than for experimenting with the world. However, Isaac had been entertaining the idea of leaving the Plain community to join the Army. The only people who knew of this were Miriam and Joshua. There was something about being in the Army that really intrigued Isaac. He had seen soldiers come through their community on tourist trips and had asked them what it was like. Many of them had been overseas and seen things Isaac only dreamed of: new worlds, new cultures, and new people. The only thing really keeping Isaac in the comfort of his community was the potential to date and marry Miriam.

"I think I'm going to ask Miriam if I can take her home," he finally said to Joshua.

Joshua chuckled, "If you hadn't said that, I would've done it."

Isaac smiled wryly. Ever since they were young, Isaac and Joshua were always in competition; to many it was even a surprise that they were such good friends. Isaac believed it was because of Miriam they were such good friends. She had broken up more than one fight and was always keeping the peace between the three of them.

"This is one thing I won't let you win."

"What? Why not?" Joshua looked affronted. "We can't even have a little friendly competition for a girl? And especially for a girl we've both liked since we were 8?"

Isaac shook his head. "Nope. I thought we had discussed this. I'm the best option for Miriam."

"Oh really? Well Mr. Hershberger doesn't seem to think so. You and I both know the rumors are for Miriam and me. I'll make a deal with you; if Miriam accepts your offer, then you can have her." Isaac shot him a skeptical look.

"That's really nice of you... but why would she say no?"

"Well, my friend, you may not realize this, but Miriam likes me better." Isaac rolled his eyes.

"Why does the world always revolve around you and your stories of a love triangle?"

Joshua held up his hands. "Hey, it's what sells these days. And I would know, since I work at a bookstore in town. But don't worry, I'll let you try to win her hand. But you and I both know, it's her father's heart you'll really have to win. So good luck." Joshua slapped him on the back again before rising from his seat. "I'm going to ask Rachel Swartz if I can take her home." He winked as he walked away. Isaac watched him leave. Rachel Swartz's father was just like Miriam's: very stubborn and wanting one person only for his daughter. In this case, that person happened to be Isaac Yoder. It occurred to Isaac in that moment that Joshua may have been trying to make him jealous, but you can't make someone jealous that doesn't even have feelings for a certain person.

Isaac sighed as he built up the courage to stand up and walk over to where Miriam was sitting. As he moved toward her, the girls around her steadily grew quieter and began speaking in more hushed tones. "Miriam," he half-squeaked as she turned to look at him. He cleared his throat before finishing his request, "May I take you home tonight?" There was suddenly a flurry of giggles from the group sitting around her.

"I'd love that," she replied sweetly. He offered his hand to help her up and began leading her toward his buggy. He had recently purchased the buggy from Rachel Swartz's father. Although "purchased" would be the wrong word, since Caleb Swartz gave it to Isaac as a sign of good faith that he would "make the right choice" in his future wife.

Isaac pushed all of that out of his mind as he helped his best friend into the carriage. He ran around the other side and got in and off they went toward Miriam's home.

About halfway there, Miriam finally spoke. "You can't take me home."

This caught Isaac off-guard for two reasons: one, she had been completely quiet until that point and it had startled him; and two, it didn't make sense.

"Why not?"

"Because," she barely whispered above the clopping of hooves, "my father will be angry with me if I bring anyone other than Joshua Hostetler home."

Neither of them spoke for a few minutes, but Isaac led the buggy toward their favorite secret spot. This spot was known only by Isaac, Miriam, and Joshua. The three of them had found multiple places to hide away from the adults over the years. This particular place was right on the edge of the community, very close to a busy road, but far enough away that it wasn't so distracting in the quiet moments. This spot was Isaac's favorite hiding spot. It was in that spot that he had tutored Miriam in her arithmetic and helped her learn how to read. It was where they had read countless Nancy Drew books in secret, and also where they would get together to talk about their fears of the future and their hopes for each other. Before life got to be about who to marry and where to work, this was where they felt the most at home. Isaac felt it was the best place to go since it had such a deep meaning for them.

As they approached the spot, he had to get out of the buggy and lead the horse to a tree where he could tie the beast up safely. Isaac picked a tree that was far enough away from the road that passersby wouldn't see the buggy and accidentally think something had happened. They were hidden quite a ways into the wood for that.

Isaac helped Miriam out of the carriage and led her through the wooded area to the clearing. It had been awhile since Isaac had been here—almost a year at least—but everything was just as he remembered it: a small circular clearing, not more than 10 feet around with three small logs around the edges of the clearing and a flat-top rock to make the fourth sitting spot. There was an evergreen tree on the north side of the clearing, and that was where they had hidden many of the "forbidden" Nancy Drew books in wooden boxes Isaac and Joshua had made in their free time at home. The entry point was on the south side, and there was a small piece of cloth with Miriam's initials on it. Isaac was never really sure why she had done that, and she had never explained herself... and that was just another reason why he loved her; she did things without anyone's approval.

The sun was almost completely gone, but the Sunday night gathering would last for some time before anybody's parents would start to get suspicious about where Isaac and Miriam were. "Remember the last time we were here together?" Miriam asked. Isaac smiled, recalling that day as if it had just happened yesterday.

"We all showed up here at the same time. You had had a rough day at school and Joshua and I just needed a break from working. We thought we could get away and just play some cards, but then you showed up." He looked into her eyes. "It was in that moment that I realized I wanted to marry you someday."

Miriam furrowed her brow as she said, "That was the day? I was a mess; I was crying like a baby—"

"No, you were wailing like an old widow." They laughed at the thought. Miriam sat down on a log.

"Yeah I was." She chuckled, but to Isaac it sounded like the birds were waking up in the morning. She began speaking again, but he could only focus on her features. Her beautiful golden hair was now freely flowing, as she had taken her head covering off after declaring that they couldn't go to her house. What she said was only mildly important to how she carried herself and how mesmerizing she was. Her green eyes fit well into her oval-shaped face. Her petite nose reminded Isaac of one of the glass baby dolls that his mother had on display at home. When she smiled, all he saw was perfectly white teeth behind full pink lips.

"Did you ever realize how beautiful you are?" He didn't even stop to think that she might have still been in the middle of a story.

"What?" She seemed a little surprised at the sudden outburst from her friend.

"You're beautiful," he declared.

She looked at him awkwardly then said, "I thought this was the time when we were supposed to talk all night long. We are basically dating, right?"

"We are talking. You're telling me stories, and I'm telling you how beautiful you are."

She scoffed. "The whole situation sounds a little one-sided to me."

Isaac shrugged. "Well, it worked. You're not telling me stories anymore."

Miriam gasped in feigned offense. "Oh, I see how it is. You don't even want to listen to how Mr. Troyer came into the shop and flirted with me? It's really quite entertaining." Isaac laughed with her. This was going to be a great night.

"Go ahead and start your story again. I'll be good and listen this time, I promise."

That night was the springboard for a whole slew of secret adventures together. Isaac and Miriam grew closer together in ways they didn't know was possible. Isaac felt like he was on the highest mountain and nothing could touch him. For the next three weeks, they would meet in their secret spot late in the evenings and talk into the middle of the night.

One night in particular, the conversation led to the future.

"Hey Isaac," Miriam started. "What do you think about the future?" She looked at him. "Do you think we end up together?" He thought long and hard and then chose his words carefully.

"I don't know what the future holds for us," he spoke slowly. "But I do know one thing." Isaac looked deep into her eyes. "I don't want to live my life without you." There was a long moment of silence as they looked into each other's eyes. Finally Miriam broke the silence again.

"Do you want to go into the Army?" Isaac looked away. The answer was, he really wasn't sure. And he told her as much.

"Those Nancy Drew books made me want to explore the world outside, and the soldiers that came through here recently made me just want to travel. So, I'm not sure if I would just travel or join the Army."

"Well," Miriam began. "You know how our Lord feels about war."

"Does He really feel that way though?" He looked up at her again. The moon was very bright that night and it made Miriam look almost angelic. He continued with his thought despite the minor distraction. "There's war and fighting all throughout the Bible. Even Jesus Himself said He came to bring a sword, and to bring families against each other."

"Do you really only want to fight because you think it's OK? Is that how you're justifying all this in your mind? Any time you take a life, that's blood on your hands that you'll have to answer for."

"Yeah, but Miriam, it's not just about the killing. It's about saving the lives of those that can't fight for themselves. Aren't you always going on about how you want to do what's right and bring justice to people's situations?"

Miriam was incredulous at this point. "Of course, but not by getting myself involved in some war and killing people. I want to help people *here,* in my community. I want to tutor young children... like you and Joshua helped tutor me." Her face softened as she leaned toward him, her voice almost a whisper. "Isn't that enough?"

Miriam was so close, Isaac would've agreed with anything she said at that point. He could feel her breath on his face, smell her sweet, natural scent. "Yeah," he breathed out, before leaning in to close the distance between his lips and hers. As soon as their lips touched, something like a fire shot through Isaac's body and he instantly wanted more. Every nerve in his system and every hair on his body seemed to be standing at attention, but in the next second, he was left breathless and confused. Miriam had pulled away.

"No," she stated firmly. "I can't." She stood to leave.

"Wait, Miriam." Isaac stood to follow her. "Don't leave. I'm sorry." He wasn't sure why he was apologizing, since he didn't really start the whole ordeal.

Miriam kept walking toward Isaac's waiting horse and buggy. "I need to leave. Please take me home."

"Wait, Miriam," he said again, more firmly this time as he reached out to grab her. She spun around, and what Isaac saw stopped him. She was crying.

"Please just take me home. I can't be with you. I can't keep playing this game of pretending to be into someone but really loving someone else."

Isaac released her arm. "Who else are you interested in?"

"It's not who I'm interested in, it's who my father *wants* me to be interested in. I can't keep pretending anymore." She looked into his eyes, and he had this sinking feeling that this might possibly be the last time he would get to talk to her for a long time. "Isaac, I love you, but if you want to date me, you *have* to get permission from my father." She turned around to continue walking toward the buggy.

"OK," he said finally. They had reached the buggy by then. "Give me a week." He reached out his hand to help her up, but she ignored it.

"Fine," she stated flatly. "Now take me home."

Three days later, he was met by his younger sister on his way out to the secret place to surprise Miriam.

"Where are you going, big brother?" Rebekah asked.

"Out," he answered curtly.

"To see Miriam?" That stopped Isaac in his tracks. He spun around.

"How did you know about that?" He asked defensively. Rebekah was 14, but sometimes Isaac swore she was his second mother. Sometimes she even caught onto things faster. This was one of those times. "You can't tell Mom and Dad about this."

"Why shouldn't I?"

"Because," he responded quickly. "If you do, they'll tell Miriam's parents and then I won't be allowed to see her anymore." Rebekah rolled her eyes.

"It's not me you have to worry about. It's all your little friends out in the fields. Everyone knows you and her have been leaving the singings together every Sunday night. Besides, it's not like his forbidding you to see her has actually stopped you. So where do you go?" She almost became a detective in that moment, and Isaac thought for sure she would pull the answer out of his eyes. As if to make sure, he looked away.

"It wouldn't be a secret place if I told you," he stated. He looked at his little sister, and in that moment, he was proud of the woman she was growing up to be. Whoever the man was that would have the honor of marrying her would be the luckiest man on the planet.

"Please, don't tell Mom and Dad. I'll tell them when the time is right."

"And when is that gonna be?" She crossed her arms as if she'd just made the best argument all day. *Wow, she is sharp,* he thought.

"Soon, I promise. I have to talk to her parents first."

"Well you better do it fast or else one of the guys in the field might let it slip. Mr. Hershberger is said to be making his rounds any day now to check on his affairs. I just worry about you, Isaac. That's all." She uncrossed her arms as her face softened. "Please don't do anything you'll regret."

Isaac smiled at her. "I promise, little sister. Thank you." He gave her a hug before heading out the door. Tonight was the night, he had decided. He would ask Miriam for forgiveness for the other night. Then he would ask if they could, in fact, go steady. Not only that, he was going to talk to Mr. Hershberger if she said yes. He felt as if he couldn't get his horse to go fast enough toward the secret spot. Sometimes the old beast had a mind of his own. As soon as he was within a shorter walking distance, he got out of the buggy and began coaxing the horse through the grass into the woods before tying it hurriedly on a tree and rushing to their spot. He had a few preparations he wanted to make before she arrived, since they had agreed on meeting at sundown after Miriam put her younger siblings to bed. He had his grandmother's wedding ring on a chain around his neck that his mother had given him on the night he turned 16.

"When you find the one you want to marry, give this to her as a token of your love," Isaac's mother had said. "Explain to her what this symbolizes, and above all, don't let her go."

These thoughts were running through his head as he walked quickly toward the clearing. As he got closer however, he heard voices. Two of them to be exact: one male, and one female. His heart started racing. Who else could know about this place? Of all the years he and his friends had been coming, not one other living human being had ever been here. He decided to hide behind one of the bushes just outside of the clearing, as he couldn't see into it because of the way he and his friends had designed it over the years. He listened intently, hoping he'd be able to recognize a voice.

His heart felt as if it dropped into his stomach and he felt all color drain from his face. He recognized both voices, and they were none other than his best friends', Miriam's and Joshua's. And they sounded happy. In a panic, Isaac forgot about stealth and all of the things he had been planning for that night as he rushed out from behind his hiding place and burst into the clearing, startling his friends.

"Isaac!" Miriam exclaimed, jumping up from her seat. "I didn't expect you tonight!"

"Didn't expect me?" He suddenly couldn't think clearly. All of the words and thoughts in his head were suddenly very jumbled. *What was going on here?* He wondered. If this is what jealousy felt like, he suddenly understood why Joseph's 10 brothers threw him into an empty cistern in the book of Genesis. "How could you not expect me? We've been meeting here almost every night for the past three weeks! I told you I had something special I wanted to tell you, and you *promised* that you would be here, alone!" Isaac's voice had reached a pitch he didn't even know existed, not to mention the volume it had gone up to. He ran his hands through his hair as he began pacing around the small clearing. He tried to get his heart rate and voice back down to a level that wouldn't arouse suspicion from anyone close by. Joshua, who had been struck mute until then, finally stood up.

"Look, we didn't mean anything by it. We were just hanging out. You can still have your time—"

"How long has this been going on?" Isaac addressed Miriam, interrupting and ignoring Joshua. His voice had now become almost calm. "Is this because of what happened the other night?"

"What?" She asked. Her eyes widened, suddenly remembering. "Oh... no!"

Joshua sighed, exasperated. "Isaac," he began. "I've tried to tell you from the start. It's about getting to know her *father.* He's the one whose heart you really have to win. He doesn't want some guy he barely knows to marry his daughter."

"Some guy he barely knows?" Isaac practically roared, forgetting all pretenses of trying to keep quiet. "I grew up with her, the same as you! We've been over to her house multiple times and had the *same* conversations with him."

Miriam attempted to be the peacemaker. "Guys, please—"

"Oh, have we now?" Joshua shouted at Isaac. "So you know what Miriam is struggling with right now? That she's still in shock from your kiss the other night? The one that *you* initiated? You know that her mother is sick and she simply can't bank on someone whose heart is set on 'traveling the world' to help take care of her. How could you be so selfish?"

Those last words struck Isaac to the heart. He looked at Miriam pleading, hoping that Joshua was wrong and that all of this was just a bad dream. Had she really been putting on a pretense all for him? "Miriam? Is what he's saying true?"

Miriam stuttered but seemed to be without many words. She looked scared, but she finally nodded.

"Well Army-man," Joshua said smugly as he folded his arms. "Looks like you didn't know her as well as you thought. Maybe you should just forget this ever happened and run on home to your little fantasy land." Just then, there was the sound of men rushing in their direction. *So much for not drawing attention,* Isaac thought, mentally kicking himself for letting his emotions get so out of control. He turned to Miriam.

"Come with me."

For the third time that night, Miriam stuttered.

"Miriam, I love you. I don't know if I could go on living without you. You mean more to me than the whole world, and there's nothing I wouldn't do for you." He moved toward her, but Joshua got between them.

"Stay away from her," he warned, his eyes bright with jealousy and hurt. The voices were getting closer.

Finally Miriam spoke a clear thought. "At one point in time, I may have loved you, but I don't know if I can love a man that can't even stand up and fight for what he thinks is right... unless it's at the end of a gun."

So this whole ordeal wasn't even about the kiss. It was about Isaac's obsession with war. Most people would've taken this as a cue to change, but Isaac took it differently.

"I'll come back for you." He looked into Miriam's eyes one more time. Those beautiful green eyes. "Then you'll know that I really do love you." She furrowed her brow in confusion.

"What? Where are you going?"

"Yeah," Joshua added, also confused. "Where *are* you going?"

The voices were almost upon them now. In a flash, he took off his grandmother's wedding ring. The thought passed through Isaac's mind that the night wasn't meant to go like this. But it was too late for that. "This is a promise, that I love you and I will come back for you. Give me three years."

"The last time you promised a certain amount of time to her, you did *nothing* to deliver on that promise," Joshua reminded him with a hint of vitriol in his voice.

"We'll see," Isaac said with what he hoped was an air of mystery in his voice. Really he was just scared of the choice he was about to make.

At that moment, the first man in the search party came through the clearing. Isaac took off running deep into the woods and farther away from everything he held dear. He thought he heard someone running after him, but Isaac was the fastest man in the community, even Joshua wouldn't be able to catch him.

For the first time in his life, he felt like he was making simultaneously the best and worst decision of his life.

And it was already killing him.

"Sgt. Yoder!"

For the first time in his life, Isaac was less than excited to have those two words in the same sentence.

"Yes sir!" He addressed his commanding officer with as much respect as he could muster. Staff Sgt. Queener was his least favorite person as of late. Ever since they had gotten into a firefight with the Islamists in Iraq a few weeks prior to returning, he would find everything wrong with anything Isaac did. Queener blamed Isaac for the fact that they had gotten into the fight in the first place, and although Isaac didn't claim Queener was wrong, he also wasn't about to take responsibility.

It was our last sweep of the town, Isaac had written down in the report. War wouldn't have been so bad if there wasn't so much red tape afterward. *We were on our way back to base when a little girl came running up to me. About 10 of us were on foot to make sure if there were any civilians, we wouldn't scare them with our big vehicles. The little girl couldn't have been more than 5 or 6, and she began speaking Farsi much faster than I could translate. I asked her to slow down, but asking her seemed to have the opposite effect. At this point, the convoy had stopped, and Cpl. Lanning had begun trying to coax me that we needed to get moving. As long as the convoy was stuck, we were practically sitting ducks.*

No sooner had he said that then shots rang out from the nearest building and instantly the little girl who had just been standing in front of me suddenly had a chest full of bullets.

At this point, Isaac had had the hardest time finishing the debrief. He couldn't understand how anyone could allow someone to die like that and continue to live a normal life. One of the psychiatrists he had talked to after coming back had said Isaac would have to find a new normal, but Isaac didn't even know what normal was since he'd left his Plain ways behind to join the Army. He did know that he was responsible for that little girl's death... as well as the death of his best friend.

Instantly a firefight broke out in that little town, but all I could do was take cover. I was the group translator, so my number one priority was to stay alive at all costs. However, I also happened to be a sharp-shooter because of my upbringing, so I managed to take a few terrorists out without anyone realizing who or what hit them.

Taking the lives of those men was nothing compared to the loss of that little girl, or my best friend, Cpl. Lanning. It wasn't until the smoke had cleared that we realized we had lost him within the first few seconds of the fight. One of those first shots had been toward him, and it was a direct hit.

Lanning's life and that little girl's were what got him, not any of the terrorists' or anyone else that might have died as a result of Isaac's actions. He still had nightmares about that day. He ran through scenarios every second of the day in the back of his mind. He remembered seeing how scared the little girl was and desperately trying to decypher what she was saying. He remembered hearing the rushed tone in his best friend's voice and—after thinking about it every night for the past month—he realized he even remembered Cpl. Lanning's last words before getting shot in the throat.

"Come on man, don't do something you'll regret."

It wouldn't have been so chilling if it wasn't so close to the last thing he had heard his sister Rebekah say to him almost 3 years ago.

"I said, did you hear me, Sergeant!?"

Queener's voice snapped him back to the present.

"Yes, sir!"

"This is a disgrace! How could you just put in a request like this? You're one of my best men!"

Maybe Isaac would've listened if he hadn't already had this conversation with himself in his head. Every decision he'd made in the past two and a half years, he'd made after deciding if hearing Staff Sgt. Queener's voice was worth it.

In this case, it was because the request that Queener was so upset about was a request to leave the Army. He needed a signature and recommendation from his commanding officer before he could get out. His time wasn't up, but it had been almost three years, and he had promised Miriam Hershberger three years. He wasn't about to renege on his promise, even if he wasn't even sure she had really waited for him.

In the middle of Queener's rant, he finally said, "I have to go see about a girl, sir."

That stopped Queener in his tracks. "Oh," he said stupidly, after a few moments. "Well, why didn't you say that to begin with?"

The next few weeks of paperwork went by at a turtle's pace, but finally Isaac was out and on his way back. He hadn't looked back at his Amish life in three years, except to think about Miriam everyday.

What would it look like now that he had had a taste of freedom and the English life? Would anybody recognize him? Would anybody care? Would Miriam care? Did she keep his grandmother's ring? What about Joshua? Did he tell everyone what Isaac had done, or did he just take Miriam for his own? He suddenly had an insatiable ache to see his friends and to give them the biggest hug ever and just weep on their shoulders.

"I should've stayed to fight," he had told his first and only friend in the Army, Cpl. Lanning. "I loved her, but I didn't know how to fight."

Lanning had leaned back to look at the ceiling before stating simply, "I don't know, the whole system sounds fishy to me. You were either going to win her or not, and if she didn't really love you, then what was the point of even 'giving it a try?' I don't know about you, but I think you leaving was the best decision you could make. Don't feel sorry for the fact that you may have just won her heart by becoming the most unreachable man she's ever known."

Isaac wasn't really sure where Lanning had gotten all of his wisdom from; Isaac had asked him one time what he thought about God and the Bible, but Lanning had just laughed at him.

"That stuff is for little kids and the weak at heart! You're better than that, Yoder."

Despite what Lanning said, Isaac held true to his faith. It was the only thing that got him out of bed in the mornings... especially after coming back from war without Lanning. He tried to push that out of his mind as he was getting closer to his hometown. Like a wave, he felt all of the shame and regret from three years ago wash over him. Coupled with the recent loss of the little girl and Lanning, the pain was almost unbearable.

He didn't know why, but he decided to stop at the secret spot, maybe to get the last look at his childhood memories. No matter how today turned out, Isaac decided, he was leaving at sundown, with or without Miriam. Not surprisingly, the clearing was empty. It was the middle of the workday, so Isaac was pretty sure it would've been void of life.

Walking into town was going to be the hardest part, Isaac had decided. Because he left, and without saying goodbye to anyone but Miriam and Joshua, he was sure a lot of people would be upset about him leaving. There weren't a lot of people at the shops because they were all in the fields or in the nearest English town working. Out of habit and homesickness, Isaac went to his parents' shop. Before his eyes had even adjusted to the dimness of the store, he was tackled by the biggest hug he had ever received.

"OH, Isaac!" It was Rebekah. Instantly, Isaac returned the hug and they just held each other and wept. Finally Isaac broke the hug.

"Where's Mom and Dad?" He asked. Rebekah looked down and began crying again.

"They're gone, Isaac." She looked back up at him. "The pain of you leaving was too much to bear. Mom passed away within a month, and Dad just passed last week.

That wave of shame and guilt suddenly felt like a tsunami of emotions. He needed to sit down. Rebekah must have noticed the color drain from his face, because she quickly pulled him to the nearest chair and began fanning him.

"I'm sorry, Isaac," she finally whispered. "I tried to find out where you were to tell you, but you made yourself almost impossible to find."

"No," Isaac finally forced out. "I'm sorry... for leaving you alone like this." He looked up at her quickly. An idea was forming in his head. "Come with me."

Rebekah was shocked. "What? Come with you? You're not coming back?"

Isaac shook his head. "I came back to get Miriam, no matter what it takes."

Rebekah looked away as her face flushed.

"What?" Isaac prodded. "Tell me."

"Well," Rebekah seemed to struggle with the right words. "She's supposed to get married tomorrow... to Joshua Hostetler."

All feelings of guilt suddenly left as adrenaline kicked in. He stood up quickly. "Little sister, I need your help."

Rebekah looked unsure, but nodded. "Okay," she said. "I'll go with you too."

Isaac was actually taken back by that. "Really?"

"Yeah, it's not like any of the available guys are all that interesting here anyway. What else is there? This shop?" She laughed sadly. Isaac moved over to her.

"Hey," he cooed as he enveloped her in his arms again. "It's alright. If you don't want to leave, I understand."

"It's not that I don't want to leave," she admitted. "It's that I don't want to forget about my parents."

Isaac pulled Rebekah back and looked into her face. "Hey. As long as we're alive, our parents will never be forgotten. We keep their memories alive by the way we live."

"But would our parents want us to just leave our community like this?"

"The better question would be, do our parents want us to be miserable in this community?"

Rebekah seemed to realize that Isaac had a point. Their parents had always been huge proponents of their children doing whatever they wanted, as long as they were happy and followed the Lord.

"Following the Lord is a lot easier out there than it is in here," Isaac added almost as an afterthought.

Rebekah furrowed her brow in suspicion. "Okay, Mr. Mind-reader. I don't need another Mother in my life."

They laughed. Isaac didn't realize how much Rebekah's laugh really did calm his nerves.

"Okay," he said, more seriously. "We need a plan to get to Miriam."

"I have an idea, but it requires a lot from you."

Nothing could be worse than the rest of my life without Miriam in it, Isaac thought as Rebekah began laying out her plan.

It was finally here. The moment Miriam had been raised and trained for all her life. Her parents were so excited, but she couldn't help feeling just a little empty. It must have shown in her face because her mother brought it up.

"Honey, what's wrong?" Ruth asked. "Today should be the happiest day of your life, but you look like your favorite doll just got stolen."

"Mama, it's just not the same without Isaac here. He was one of my best friends too, and it's hard knowing that he can't be here to see this."

"I know, honey," her mother said sympathetically. "But it might just be better this way. You know Daddy never liked Isaac much anyway."

Miriam sighed heavily. That didn't make it any better, but she had to give credit to Ruth for trying. She wasn't supposed to get married until later that evening, because there were a lot of preparations going into this day. She wouldn't even be in her dress until midday, when they would start preparing her makeup and hair for the ceremony later on.

"You look beautiful," a familiar voice said. Miriam spun around to see who it was, half hoping it was Isaac Yoder, since she had just dreamed last night that he had rode into town on a horse and swept her away from this whole world. It was her father, Jacob, and he looked the proudest she had ever seen him. She smiled wide.

"Thank you, Daddy," she curtsied playfully as he moved into the room to give her a hug.

"I'm so proud of you, Miriam Joy," his voice sounded husky, like he was holding back tears. "So proud."

She pulled back a little bit to look into his face. It occurred to her that this was the beginning of a new era for her father, since she was the first of five girls that would be getting married over the course of the next ten years.

"I'm just glad Mama gets to be here to see this," Miriam said thankfully.

"Mmm," was all Jacob could force out, as tears were now flowing freely. He kissed his eldest daughter on the head and left the room. Miriam wasn't sure how she would feel if Isaac did show up today, but after seeing her father cry, she didn't know if she'd be able to bring herself to leave him like Isaac seemed to do with so much ease three years ago. He had made it look so easy, but she could hardly bear the thought of leaving her family alone for one minute.

Or so she hoped.

That hope is what Isaac and Rebekah were doing their best to play on. Rebekah hadn't become extremely close to Miriam over the past few years, but she knew enough to know that Miriam would most likely leave with Isaac if he showed up and asked her to. True to Lanning's prediction, Miriam had grown more fond of Isaac... even to the point of intentionally waiting exactly three years to get married.

Isaac saw it as a test of his love; would he be willing to potentially ruin his best friends' wedding if it meant winning the love of his life? Without a thought, Isaac knew the answer was yes. He had made too many mistakes in his life to let this one try to rule him.

Rebekah told Isaac that Miriam would be going to the flower shop alone right before heading back to her house to get dressed for the wedding. That would be the best time to talk to her.

True to predictions, Miriam walked into the flower shop alone. Isaac made no time at all in getting there. He was destined to do this long before the wedding.

"Miriam Hershberger," he declared before his eyes had adjusted from the sun outside to the darker interior. By the time they had, he realized he was standing face to face with none other than Miriam.

In another lifetime, he might have taken a step back and apologized for standing so close to her. This was not another lifetime. For the first time in three years, Isaac smelled that sweetness emanating off of her. She had pulled herself so close to him just like that night in the secret spot, but this time Isaac made the move. He pulled her in tight and kissed her fully on the lips. It was like fire and ice, burning and refreshing all at the same time.

It was just like Miriam's dream! Not only had Isaac returned, but he was there to take her away. This kiss confirmed it. She pulled herself as close as she could to him, determined to never let him go. Finally, he pulled himself away, drinking in every detail of her with his eyes.

"Come away with me."

"What about Joshua? And my father?"

Isaac was undaunted. "What about them? Are you living your life for them... or for yourself?" His voice was barely a whisper, but to Miriam it seemed as if he was shouting. He was shouting, *I love you! I desire you! Come away with me! Never look back!*

"Do you know what day it is?" Miriam asked him. He smiled.

"May 28th. Three years to the day that I told you I would be back. You waited for me."

"I knew you would come." She pulled the ring off from around her neck. "This is for you; it's a symbol of my undying love and devotion to you. I don't know why I ever treated you the way I did, Isaac. I—"

He put his finger on her lips. "Whatever happened in the past is in the past. Now is the only moment worth living for." He looked deep into her eyes. "Will you come with me right now?"

"Yes!" There wasn't a second thought in Miriam's mind. She didn't care what anyone thought or what would happen to her. She was in the arms of the man she had always truly loved.

Getting Miriam to leave without saying goodbye to anyone was the hardest thing to do, so Isaac compromised. They both went to see Joshua.

Joshua was at the church getting preparations ready. Normally he wouldn't be doing anything, but he wanted to surprise her. Then he turned around and saw what seemed like two ghosts coming down the aisle toward him. As soon as Joshua saw them coming, he knew that his life with Miriam was over. He had finally been bested by his best friend, Isaac Yoder. They not only looked happy, but also like they were about to leave.

"You're leaving with my girl?" Joshua said with a twinge of hurt in his voice.

"Come with us, Joshua," Miriam pleaded. Joshua only shook his head.

"A love triangle might sell in the world of books, but it doesn't work in real life." Joshua put his hand out toward Isaac. Isaac took it. "You bested me, old friend. Now don't mess it up."

Isaac smiled. He could tell by the way Joshua responded that even he saw this coming. "Thank you, old friend. I do wish you would come with us, but you're right about the whole love triangle. Besides, I think Rachel Swartz still likes you." Isaac winked. Joshua only smiled.

"Get out of here before I change my mind. Besides, you can't just take the whole community with you. There would be no one to make awesome tourist attractions to intrigue soldiers coming back from war."

Isaac had to laugh at Joshua's attempt to be funny. He was taking this better than Isaac expected, and that was all that really mattered in that moment.

"Goodbye, Joshua Hostetler."

"Goodbye, Isaac Yoder. Don't get too crazy out there. Goodbye, Miriam. I hope your life is all of the happiness you're wishing for and more. You deserve it."

Miriam smiled. "Thank you so much." She went to hug Joshua, but he pulled away.

"Don't make this any harder than it already is," he warned. Now Isaac could see that he really was hurt. It broke his heart that it had to end like this, but he was glad that Miriam would be with him.

"I'll write to you from time to time," Isaac said. "The Hardy Brothers need some new adventures anyway."

They shared a moment of camaraderie before Isaac and Miriam turned and walked out of the church and into their new lives.

They met Rebekah at the secret place. "I talked to your dad," she addressed Miriam. "He cried. He wanted me to give you this. I guess he always knew this was coming." She pulled out a small book: her grandmother's diary. She had never been allowed to open it, but she had been told stories from it.

"I guess he was going to give it to you at the wedding, but since he'll never see you again..." Rebekah trailed off.

There were a few moments of no talking before Isaac finally said, "Let's go. It's time to start our new life together."

He smiled as he put his arms around his sister and his lifelong love. As bittersweet as the parting was, it was the best decision he had ever made. In that moment, there was nowhere else he'd rather be than in the arms of the woman he loved.

MY AMISH HOME

SARAH HAMPTON

It was cold for a mid-June morning. Anna stood by the county road unaffected by the cool breeze. After all, she was used to the hard winters that Seymour could bring. Despite the sun barely rising, the fields were already chirping and buzzing with life. Life started early in the countryside. Anna fidgeted with her luggage. She was not used to doing nothing during the time of day meant for *work*. However, her cousin picking her up had balked at the idea of doing anything before 8 AM, so here she stood and waited on a Friday morning.

She didn't mind waiting. In fact, she was trying to soak in all facets of her familiar home while she could. It was hard to believe that she would be hundreds of miles away by tonight. *Hundreds of miles.* Whisked away by some sort of electric transportation to a new land. Anna had never ridden in a car before. In her opinion, they made far too little noise and could not be trusted. Still, there had to be a reason for Rumspringa to be a time-honored tradition, right? She had heard of girls who never came back. She didn't understand how anyone could turn on their origins. Her parents had told her they would understand whatever she chose to do, but it seemed clear to Anna that they would prefer she stay. After all, they were getting older. She frequently worried about her father working in the field with his bad back. She had always helped him with his work despite her mother's insistence she learn to do "ladylike" crafts instead. As a kid, she would insist on going to the field with her father and carry his tools around, which did not help whatsoever. When she got older, she proved she could work as long and hard as her brothers. Her mother didn't chide her as often now, but she never gave up offering opportunities. *Wouldn't you like to help me cook for this week's market? I could use some help with this quilt. Oh Anna, don't wipe mud on your dress.* She smiled as she thought of her parents. She would be there for them as soon as she returned. She wouldn't allow herself to be dazzled by city lights and electric buggies.

Speaking of which, her electric buggy was supposed to be here by now.

"Where are you, Brittany?" she mumbled absentmindedly as she tapped her wrist.

There was nothing there, of course. She and her friends had seen English people at the markets angrily tapping their digital watches as they demanded punctuality. This had quickly caught on with the children, and it was now the standard among her friends to sarcastically tap their wrists when informing another person of their lateness. Some Amish did wear purely mechanical watches, but it was fairly rare among their order.

She wouldn't see her friends for quite some time. She sat down on her luggage case as she thought about their gathering last night. She was the only one leaving today. The others were either too young or had already returned from their Rumspringas. So, of course, it was an endless torrent of questions and advice. As the night passed, discussion turned to how things would go for Anna.

"I bet Anna will find some rich prince and he'll whisk her away to his foreign castle," giggled her friend Collette.

"Oh, I would never do that," replied Anna, trying to hide a smile.

Collette followed up, unabashed. "Uh huh. And when you do, do you think he'll let us come visit you?"

"Actually," intoned Catherine, "Anna is far too focused on her studies for that sort of thing. If she doesn't watch out, she'll die an old maid."

Anna laughed, but recognized some truth to the statement. "And is that such a bad thing? It seems like wealthy, foreign princes are often in need of old maids. So, I'll still be in a castle."

Collette pounced on this wording, just like Anna knew she would. "Oh, so you admit you're looking for a prince? My, my. I wonder what Elijah would say to that?"

Elijah Beiler was Anna's neighbor and longtime friend. As children, they had quickly struck up a solid friendship due to their mutual hobbies of playing in mud and climbing trees. He was her partner in crime for every dirty, *boyish* activity her friends didn't want to do. They had remained close as they entered their teens. As one could imagine, this spawned lots of teasing and rumors among Anna's girlfriends, but she never allowed herself to take them seriously. If Elijah had any romantic feelings towards her, wouldn't he have shown them by now? After all, frog catching was hardly the courtship material of fantasy novels.

Anna tried to remain deadpan, but couldn't hide the slightest twinge of annoyance in her voice. "I imagine if he had anything to say about it at all, he would had stayed around longer tonight."

She knew it was unfair to blame him for leaving early. He had to help his father pack for the market tomorrow. Still, the petty side of her felt a little disappointed. It was quite likely this would be the last time they would see each other in a long time. Couldn't he sacrifice a little bit of sleep to stay around longer? Truthfully, her feelings for him had changed over time. As they developed into adults, she had come to view him in a way she didn't think he reciprocated. Her friends never gave up an opportunity to tease her about his boyish good looks, his olive skin, or his muscular, strong body built from working the farm since he could hold a hoe. No one ever believed her, but she didn't really care about that. She liked him because of how close they were. She had shared a lot with him and he always accepted her the way she was. In addition, though Elijah was not a purposefully funny man, he always made her laugh with his deadpan, straightforward statements. Anna had trouble imagining developing the same level of bond with another person, let alone another man. Besides, who else would want a girl who wipes mud on her dresses?

Anna stopped her thoughts there. She was supposed to be annoyed at him. The sun was fully shining now. A few strands of her dark red hair obstructed her view. She blew at them forcefully like they somehow represented Elijah. They fluttered a little bit and fell back. She blew at them again—harder this time.

"You know, if you keep doing that, you'll feel lightheaded."

Anna was never one to scream, but the sudden male voice made her jump. She turned around to see Elijah climbing over the fence on the side of the road toward her. She briefly felt a moment of panic about the thoughts she had been having. She knew she had an occasional habit of thinking out loud. If Elijah had heard anything, it didn't show on his face. He walked up to her, took off his hat, and ran his hand through his dark hair while he eyed her worriedly.

"Are you okay? Your face is a little red. It could be the oxygen deprivation."

Anna quickly composed herself. "Eli. My face is perfectly fine, thank you very much. What are you doing here?"

She looked behind him. There were only cows munching grass in the field. "How did you even get here anyway?"

Elijah blinked. "I walked."

"From the market? That must have been five miles."

"I wanted to see you off."

Anna was pleasantly surprised but didn't let it show. "Why didn't you see me off last night then, like everyone else?" she snapped. "And what about your father's market stall?"

Elijah was unfazed. "It was a slow day and I asked if I could leave early. And, well, you seemed to be enjoying time with your friends last night and we wouldn't have had time to talk."

This was an unexpectedly soft sentiment from Elijah, and Anna couldn't think of a quick response.

"I'm just glad I caught you before you left," he added.

Anna tried to hold on to her annoyance. "Well, you almost didn't. I should be gone by now."

"With Brittany picking you up? You'd be lucky if she's awake by now." He rubbed his right leg distractedly. "Plus, I angered a few cows and had to take an unexpected detour."

At this, Anna had to laugh. She stepped forward to embrace him and they sat and made small talk for a few passing minutes. Something popped into her mind.

"So, what did you want to talk to me about last night?

She could see him visibly tense and his countenance changed. There was a small pause before he answered.

"It's just that you're leaving, and I won't see you for a while..." His speaking patterns were too slow and steady for stuttering, but Anna could sense indecision whirring in his brain.

"Yes. And?"

Elijah continued, "I thought I should tell you..." He paused to think. "That you shouldn't..."

Anna was thoroughly confused. "I shouldn't leave? I shouldn't talk to strangers? I shouldn't learn to dance the can-can?"

Elijah was stone-faced but Anna could sense an inner sigh. Whatever he wanted to say, he wouldn't be saying it today.

"You shouldn't forget to say your morning prayers, that's all." He stood and looked down the road. "It seems as if your cousin does have some work ethic. I believe I hear her car."

With that, he gave a goodbye hug and went on his way. Anna couldn't see a car in the distance, but Elijah always had weirdly good hearing. And she couldn't, for the life of her, think of what he possibly wanted to tell her.

—-

Sure enough, after a short while, Anna could hear the familiar sound of Brittany's red Toyota Camry traveling down the dirt road at breakneck speeds. When it arrived, Anna jumped back and let out an exasperated huff. The window rolled down to reveal her ecstatic cousin, designer sunglasses placed on her perfectly styled brunette hair to show her green eyes twinkling with excitement.

"Do all English people drive like that?" cried Anna.

Brittany laughed, "I'm the best driver in Chicago! You haven't seen the half of it."

Anna sighed. "At this rate, I fear I won't even make it to the city."

Brittany winked and got out to help Anna with her luggage. "Don't be such a worrywart! Trust me. You are in great hands."

She stopped to wave at Anna's family approaching behind her. They had heard the car too and were coming to say goodbye. "Now, hurry up and get in! We have a schedule to keep, you know."

Anna's littlest brother Jakob, with the energy only bestowed upon the quite young, was the first to arrive. He came to a sudden stop upon closer look at the strange large machine of transportation. The look of awe on her brother's face made Anna giggle. She remembered the first time she had seen an "electric buggy".

"Jakob! Don't even think about climbing on that car!" shouted Anna's mother, Abigail.

"But, how else am I going to ride it?" asked the confused 6-year old.

"I'll explain it to you later, son. Get back now. It's time for Anna to go."

The young boy frowned, stepped back, and asked with sadness, "You'll come back soon, right Anna?"

Anna picked him up and held him tightly. "Of course I will. I'll have presents for you too!"

At the talk of presents, Jakob immediately perked up and was back to his cheerful self again. Abigail smiled as each of Anna's siblings said their goodbyes. Her father approached and handed her a small parcel. She looked inside. It was a blue and white quilt she had made when she was 11 years old.

"It might get chilly in Chicago. You wouldn't want to catch a cold." Her father said gently.

Anna smiled gratefully and touched her father's hand. "I'll bring it back with me soon."

—-

The drive to Chicago seemed to go by quickly as she and Brittany caught each other up on their lives. They made several stops along the way, as Brittany saw things that caught her fancy. Soon after they arrived in the city, discussion came to Anna's new job.

"So, basically you'll just assist with office work. You'll organize files, help with scheduling, and basically anything else Dr. Jamison wants." Brittany explained in her trademark fast pace, no wear in her voice even after hours of nonstop talking.

Anna nodded, "Is that what you do?"

Brittany laughed. "No. I don't even technically work there. My firm handles their marketing campaigns. You'll love your coworkers though. They're good friends of mine. You'll like Dr. Jamison too, and maybe his son."

Anna nodded again, mesmerized by the electric glow of the world passing by outside. The sun was beginning to set and the city's neon lights grew brighter in comparison. By the time they arrived at Brittany's condo, the night had completely settled. Anna was feeling exhausted from the ride, but Brittany didn't show any signs of stopping as she unlocked and opened the door.

"Ta da! I didn't have a chance to get a key copied for you, so we'll have to do that tomorrow. Oh, there's the cutest coffeeshop down the street from the locksmith. I've been meaning to try it. We can go there together! Of course, first we'll have to get you some new clothes at the shopping mall."

Anna yawned and sat down. "The shopping mall?"

Brittany gave Anna a bemused look. She knew the Amish knew more about outside life than most people thought. She was always careful not to be condescending. "It's like... A big farmer's market." Brittany said slowly.

Anna laughed, "I know what a shopping mall is. I already have clothes though."

This remark got an alarmed look from Brittany. "Oh, but you don't plan on wearing those out here do you?"

"Well, yes I did."

Brittany spirits looked visibly doused. "Well, okay. I'm sure the clinic has a dress code, though, so we should still get you some office clothing..."

Anna relented a bit. "Oh yes. But afterwards, perhaps we could go shopping for some fun modern styles? You know how clueless I am towards fashion."

Brittany's face lit up instantly, "That would be great! It'll be so much fun. In fact, I may know a mall that's still open now..." She said, already checking her smartphone for opening hours.

"Actually," Anna said quickly, giving a more exaggerated yawn this time, "I'm feeling pretty tired. Do you mind if we just stay here tonight?"

And so they did. Brittany made a pasta dinner for the two of them using packaged foods Anna had never seen. They spent the rest of the night watching old movies. Anna concluded her first night in the city falling asleep on the couch, not as enthused by the technological marvel of television as Brittany had hoped.

—-

The rest of the weekend passed in what seemed like a whirlwind to Anna. There seemed to be no end to the amount of things Brittany wanted to show Anna. They had been friends since they were very young, and got along effortlessly. The city girl took Anna shopping for clothes first, of course. After hours of trying on dresses, tops, bottoms, accessories, and what seemed like every shoe in the store, they finally found a wardrobe that was chic enough for Brittany and sensible enough for Anna.

Anna found that her cousin's energetic nature was infectious, and soon was genuinely excited to do the many things suggested to her. Naturally, this delighted Brittany. More hours were spent meeting her friends and Anna's new coworkers. They seemed to truly be interested in Anna's stories of her Amish life and her observations of the city. During mealtimes, Brittany seemed to insist Anna try a new style of food every time. Anna preferred her mother's cooking, but still marveled at the variety available.

Sunday night, Brittany handed Anna a brand-new smartphone and explained how to use it. She had already added the number for her phone, emergency services, and local restaurants to the contacts. She had also created a Facebook account for Anna. The account had 7 "friends," which Anna imagined to be a lot. Brittany then gave Anna her credit card with Anna's name on it.

When Anna protested, Brittany waved it off and said "I don't have any siblings and I don't plan to have children any time soon. I make more money than I need. I don't have anyone else to care for, and you're like a little sister to me. I leave town pretty frequently, so I want you to be covered. Just in case."

Anna kept the card in her new wallet but told herself she would only use it in emergencies.

—-

Compared to the pace of the weekend, her office job seemed to be in slow-motion. She had carried a few boxes and retrieved a few files, but a large part of her time was spent sitting in a comfortable leather chair. Accustomed to the hard labor of working her family's farm, Anna kept asking if there was more work to be done.

Her coworkers found this funny. "You are working. You're sitting there, smiling at patients who come in, and telling them where to sit. This business would fall apart without you. You are the backbone of this operation, not Dr. Jamison," they said. Overhearing this comment, Dr. Jamison laughed and assured Anna she was doing perfectly fine.

The bell dinged and a tall, well-dressed young man with neatly groomed blond hair entered.

"Hello!" enthused Anna. "Please have a seat. Do you have an appointment with Dr. Jamison?"

The young man gave Anna a smile. "I am Dr. Jamison."

"Not yet you're not," her boss's voice interjected before Anna could react. "Your board results haven't come in yet."

The young man approached Anna's desk so he could more clearly see Dr. Jamison behind her. "Yes, father. I'm aware of that. I'm sure I know what the results are, though. Are you thinking I could have failed?" Now that he was closer, Anna could detect a hint of cologne. The subtly pleasant scent contrasted with the edge in his words.

Dr. Jamison, who had been very open and friendly to Anna, didn't even look up from his paperwork and spoke with an admonishing tone which she sensed was very familiar to this young man. "Yes, Christopher. There is always a chance. One day you'll see beyond your ego and realize that."

The young man took a step back and gave a light shrug at Anna. "Very well. Not Dr. Jamison, then. Just Chris, for the moment. I came to drop off a few documents for the *doctor*. I need to speak with him about them."

"Not now, Christopher. I have to prepare these files and then I have patients. Come back at 4:30," came the reply.

To this, the young man gave a thin smile and left without another word, leaving Dr. Jamison shaking his head. Anna offered no comment, but was surprised at how tense English families could be.

—

At 5 PM came closing time. Again, it surprised Anna to end the workday so long before sun down. Her new coworkers said their goodbyes, already treating her like they were the oldest of friends. Anna sat and waited on the outside deck for Brittany's car. She was a bit late, but that was not uncommon. A true sign of a newcomer to the city, Anna spent the time looking at the cityscape and passing cars instead of playing on her phone.

About fifteen minutes later, Chris showed up looking for his father. Approaching the building, he could see the lights in the office were already dark and sighed. He walked up to the door, not seeming to notice Anna.

She spoke up. "Oh, I think he's already gone. I'm sorry."

She almost instantly regretted saying anything. Based on her previous interaction with this young man, she expected him to offer a snide comment or disparaging look. However, he just sighed again and sat down in a chair across from her.

"I figured he would be. He knows I have lessons until 5. Lunchtime is the only time we were both supposed to be free." He ran his thin fingers through his hair, partially ruining the perfect streaks.

"Why did he tell you to come back at 4:30 then, if he knows you can't make it?"

Chris massaged his temples. "It's his way of saying he's too busy for me."

Anna was surprised to see a vulnerable side to what she had originally perceived as a highly-strung, egotistical man. Having nothing else to do, she decided to probe further.

"Isn't he proud of you, though? You're going to be a doctor." She hesitated before adding the next part but went ahead. "You don't even look old enough to be one."

The young man looked up at Anna. For a moment, she feared she had angered him but he simply laughed and said "I'm sorry, what is your name again? I suppose I've already offered you mine."

Anna offered out her hand, "I'm Anna. I'm new here."

Chris shook her hand. "Chris Jamison. I can tell you're new." His hands were pale but surprisingly warm.

Anna giggled and he continued, "To answer your question, I graduated from university early and went to medical school afterwards. The medical board also thought I was too young, but agreed to allow me to take the examinations, provided I don't practice until next year."

"Next year?"

"When I turn eighteen."

This confused Anna. "So that means you're only..."

"Seventeen, yes. I get these questions a lot."

Chris was only one year older that she was. She took in his facial structure again. He was older than he looked, then. She probed further. "So you're pretty smart, huh?"

This prompted a laugh. "Some might say so. Others, not so much. In truth, I've just always been a very curious person. I read a lot of books as a child."

This seemed unexpectedly modest to Anna from a man characterized as egotistical by his own father. She felt some admiration for what he had achieved at such a young age. "Wow," she mumbled, thinking about her own life.

He leaned back in his chair, his previous melancholy mood forgotten. "So did my father hire you to guard his door? You look a bit too nice for that."

Anna checked the time on her new phone. "Well, I'm waiting for my cousin to come pick me up, but she's late and she hasn't called."

Chris leaned over a little to look at her phone. "Has she texted? You have an unread message."

"Has she what? Oh!" Anna had forgotten about this feature on her phone. She pulled up her messages, and sure enough, she saw one from Brittany.

Hi Anna!!! How was your first day at work? I can't wait to hear about it. My meeting got delayed and I won't be able to get free for several hours! Sorry. Go out with Mike and Kelly. I'll call you when I'm done! XOXOXO"

This message was interspersed with curious yellow cartoon faces, which Anna took to represent exaggerated emotions. Mike and Kelly were her new coworkers. She looked up at their parking spaces. Empty.

Chris took in the look on her face. "It seems that she won't be here for a while."

Anna got up. "Yeah, she's in a meeting. It's okay. I can walk home."

At this, Chris laughed and shook his head.

"What?" said Anna, defensively.

"No offense, but that would be like a puppy walking in the Amazon. You look curious and trusting. That's a dead giveaway you're new to the city. A perfect target for predators."

The last word brought images of bears and wolves to Anna's mind, but then she understood what he meant.

He pressed on, "Plus, I'm willing to bet you're not quite sure how to get home anyway."

That was true. Anna hesitated. "Well..."

Chis stood up and started walking down the front steps. "Come on, I'll drive you."

Anna stood still. "What?"

Christ kept walking. "I'll drive you. You don't want to take a taxi. They charge double rates to people who look like tourists, which you do. My father clearly isn't here, so I have some free time."

Anna followed him a little bit so she could hear what he was saying. She didn't want to be impolite. However, she wasn't sure if she could trust this complicated young man. As Chris opened the driver door to his sleek black Mercedes, he turned to look at her.

"Come on. You can tell your cousin what you're doing. You'll be perfectly safe."

That's right, Anna thought. *Didn't Brittany say she knew Dr. Jamison's son?* She looked up at the sky. It was cloudy, as it often was in

Chicago. She didn't particularly feel like being caught in the rain. She shrugged internally and ran towards Chris's car. *In the spirit of running around, right?*

—-

Not long after they began driving, drops of rain started to appear on the windshield. Anna breathed an internal sigh of relief. Although she didn't think she displayed any outward emotion, Chris seemed to know what she was thinking and gave her a smile.

"Where do you live again?" Chris asked, pulling up the GPS on his dashboard.

I guess it would be silly to hide that now, Anna thought. "In the 600 North Fairbanks Condos. Have you been there?"

"No, but soon I will," he said, typing in the address with soft, precise touches.

Anna watched him. "You know, I wouldn't know personally, but I've heard it's bad to text and drive."

Chris looked and her and shrugged. "You do it, then."

Anna looked over at the glowing screen on his dashboard. After some trouble, she managed to get the device to do what she wanted. She looked over at Chris, quite pleased with herself.

Chris gave a light chuckle but didn't comment. After a short pause, he spoke again. "So how was your first week in English society?"

She was disappointed "I thought I set up the GPS correctly."

"Oh no, you did well. See?" He pointed to the screen where it said her address.

"Then how—" she started.

"Your clothes. It's your first time wearing them. The scent of the clothing shop is still on them. I didn't think you would have chosen that perfume for yourself, it's a bit bold for someone like you. Plus, you've already told me you're from out of town."

He paused to sip water out of a glass bottle before continuing. "It's not just a new outfit for a new job, either. Every time you lean over, you're instinctively rolling up sleeves that aren't there. You're not used to wearing short-sleeve clothing, but your arms are still tan. Very unusual for a city dweller."

Anna felt a little embarrassed, for some reason. "Maybe I'm just from the country," she challenged.

Chris nodded, "Your accent is slightly southern, but you're not used to any sort of machinery. You subconsciously hold your breath when I accelerate quickly. And why would a girl your age move to Chicago to live with her cousin? You're too young for college. I'm guessing you're on your Rumspringa. How is it?"

Anna took this in. "But how did you know it was the first week?"

He laughed. "Because you check your phone very infrequently for a millennial. My father's clinic has had Amish workers before, and that usually changes after the first week."

Anna found his statements to seem somewhat presumptuous, even though they were factual and things she would freely tell people. "It actually hasn't been a week," she huffed.

This tone made Chris glance over at her again. "I'm sorry. That made you uncomfortable, didn't it?" he mused. "Sometimes I get excited and get ahead of myself. Maybe I do need to see past my own ego."

She decided to encourage this softer side of him. "It's okay. It was true."

He responded with a smile and they drove in silence for a while.

A thought occurred to Anna and she spoke up again. "Did you notice anything else?"

This time, he waited before answering. He pointed to a road sign for a bakery. "You're probably hungry," he finally offered.

Anna hadn't eaten since breakfast and she suddenly felt the pangs of hunger. She looked at her new watch. There was plenty of time before Brittany got off work. She agreed to go eat.

"Did you just guess?" she asked.

"Yes," said Chris, pulling into the parking lot. He decided not to tell Anna he had trained himself to guess a person's last meal from the smell of their breath.

—-

Anna thought about Chris and the bakery as she opened the door to Brittany's condo. She had had an unexpectedly good time. The bakery turned out to be owned by Italians. It was undoubtedly Anna's favorite place in the city so far. She expected herself to return soon. She smiled as she remembered the welcoming nature of the middle-aged couple that owned it. They had greeted her and Chris like old friends and seemed genuinely sorry to see them leave. Truthfully, it reminded Anna of how people were in her hometown. Apparently, Chris was a regular customer there.

She had learned a lot about Chris. As they told each other about their lives, they discovered that they shared a surprising amount of interests. They both loved classical art, piano music, and reading. Chris, who had initially come across as cold and standoffish, was an extremely passionate person. As he had said earlier, he was very curious. This applied to virtually everything. He told her about various authors and their differing viewpoints on a broad spectrum of subjects, including astronomy, medicine, philosophy, art, history, theatre, and literature. She didn't understand all of the terminology he used, but as a curious person herself, it was intrinsically interesting. Chris was pleasantly surprised when she brought up her own theories and questions. He was used to people nodding along and feigning interest. Anna appreciated how he answered her questions and explained things simply without seeming condescending.

When she mentioned this, he said "Einstein believed that if a person couldn't explain something simply, then they didn't understand it well enough." This was followed by a quick list of little-known Einstein facts.

They had stayed much later than she had expected, but Brittany had informed her via text that she had stopped to get a few drinks with friends after work anyway. As Anna rested in one of Brittany's brightly-colored lounge chairs, she was surprised to find that the smile on her face was from thoughts of Chris as much as thoughts of the bakery. She thought fondly of his enthusiasm and charm. *Are all men in the city like this?* she wondered.

As she was thinking about taking a shower, Brittany burst into the room. Her cousin changed out of her office clothing in what Anna thought must be record-breaking speed, all the while talking about her day. In less than a minute, Brittany was reclined next to Anna, dressed in evening wear and sipping a glass of Zinfandel.

"Anyway, enough about me. Your first day at work! How was it? I'm sorry I couldn't pick you up. I'm sure you were okay with Mike and Kelly, though. I think they're dating now. But I thought Mike was gay? Maybe he just dresses well. Which one drove you home?"

She paused to take a drink and Anna picked this opportunity to speak before more questions came.

"My first day went really well. And, actually, Chris drove me home." She realized that she had forgotten to tell Brittany with who gave her a ride.

Brittany paused mid-sip. "Chris Jamison?"

"Yes, him."

She looked up at Anna, her eyes bristling with the excitement of possible gossip. "He's cute, isn't he? Tell me everything."

So Anna did, starting from his office visit to the bakery to the ride home. Brittany listened intently, nodding along to every sentence. When Anna finished, her cousin beamed at her.

"Oh, Anna, that's great! I'm so glad my meeting ran late, now! I wonder, would that be divine intervention? I did throw a penny into the fountain at the mall." She scratched her chin.

Anna wrinkled her brow. "What?"

Brittany sat up and looked at Anna. "It sounds like you two hit it off. He clearly likes you."

Anna was still confused. "You mean, romantically?"

"Yes, romantically! He *likes* likes you. He's usually very involved with himself and doesn't talk much to anyone else. You must have caught his eye. I knew buying that blouse was the right decision!" Brittany looked like she was on the verge of squealing.

This seemed doubtful to Anna. "Well, I don't know about that..."

Brittany went into a neutral expression. "Oh, you don't like him?"

Anna hadn't even considered this. She had just met him, after all. *Life moves so fast in the city*, she thought.

"It's not that. I just..." she stopped, not knowing what to say. She had only felt that way about Elijah, before. She thought about the last time she'd seen him. Although it made her stomach clench a bit, she decided to tell Brittany about her feelings for her long-time neighbor and friend. After she was done, she felt as if a weight had been lifted from her chest.

Brittany nodded, taking this in. "I'd wondered if anything was going on between you two."

"Well, there's not. I don't think he feels that way about me and I don't know anything about Chris."

Brittany stood up and stretched, finally seeming to slow down. "Well, go out on a few dates with Chris and see how you like him. You can always stop."

"Go out?"

Brittany turned to look Anna in the eye. "He did ask you out somewhere, right?"

Anna thought about this. "Well, he did mention taking me to the theatre this weekend."

She told Brittany more about it. As she finished, Brittany excitedly spoke. "That's a date!"

"Is it?" Anna said, flabbergasted.

"Yes! We'll have to decide what you wear! Oh, so little time to shop."

As Brittany started talking to herself about outfit possibilities, Anna thought about what she wanted to do. She was unsure about dating anyone, but she found that she was quite excited at the thought of seeing Chris again. *I'll go,* she decided, *and then we'll see what happens.*

—-

The week passed uneventfully except for the weather cooling unexpectedly. The condo was well heated, but it made Anna feel a little warmer on the inside when she slept in the quilt her father gave her. Then, the weekend came and Chris took her to the theatre. The production was *Les Miserables*. She had read the book before, but was awestruck to see the plot re-enacted by the characters' singing voices. The main character, Jean Valjean, was played by a handsome man with a passionate voice. When the story ended, Anna was surprised to find a single tear rolling down her left cheek. Chris, not taking his eyes off the stage, offered her a handkerchief.

As they were leaving the theatre, it was chilly and Chris draped his dark blazer over her shoulders. They talked about the play as they walked back to the car and on the drive back. They shared their favorite parts and he told her about the history involved in the plot. He drove her to the front entrance of the condos and exited the car to open the door for her. He held her gently by the shoulders when she stood up.

"So, what did you think?" he asked.

She didn't think he was talking about the play. "I really had a good time," she replied quietly. She meant it, and offered him a warm smile.

He returned it. "Would you like to go out again next weekend?"

She thought about it. Despite what she discussed with Brittany, she wasn't completely comfortable with courting someone she just met. In her home community, courtships were serious business, and people only began them after knowing the person for some time. However, it seemed that the English use dating as a way of getting to know someone. She really hadn't felt uncomfortable tonight at all. In fact, she was surprised at how relaxed Chris made her.

"Yes," she said, smiling wider. The smile hadn't faded by the time she walked into her condo. Brittany was, of course, ecstatic.

—-

As it turned out, she saw him before that weekend. The following Wednesday, he had come in to see his father after work and they went out for coffee afterwards. There was a Starbucks coffeehouse on the street of her workplace, but Chris had turned his nose up at that. He took her to a hole-in-the-wall place with excellent pastries and beautiful latte art. She had always liked dark coffee, but she found that she was becoming attached to the more ornate espresso drinks popular among English girls.

They still went out that weekend. They went out next weekend too. The following month flew by as they saw each other more frequently. She felt as if he was trying to take her to everywhere in the city. They went hiking, boating, and even jet skiing once. He was teaching her how to drive, and she was doing surprisingly well. He tried to sign her up for a gym, but she just couldn't see why people would pay money to lift heavy objects.

She remembered one time in particular. They had planned to go see an outdoor concert in the evening, but a sudden downpour had caused the band to reschedule. He suggested they go to his house and she agreed. She discovered he lived slightly outside of city limits. They were soon pulling into the driveway of an enormous building on top of a hill.

"What part of this is yours?" she asked, craning her head to see how high the manor went.

He laughed. "All of it. Well, my family technically owns it, but I'm the eldest of two heirs."

He explained that his family members were mostly wealthy businessmen in the pharmaceutical industry. Only he and his father were currently doctors. His family has supported him through medical school, but he wanted to eventually break off and make his own living. This was not a popular decision among his family, and led to tension between him and his father.

Chris opened the front door for Anna and she walked in. She took in the beautiful architecture of the convex ceiling. Chris strolled in to the dimly lit area and pointed to a piano at the far end of the living room. It was illuminated by the light of a large window. Anna could see droplets of the rain sticking to the window, casting wide shadows within the building.

"This is where I've been spending a lot of time since I finished school," he said, sitting down in front of it. He gestured to Anna to sit next to him.

The music he played was dark and haunting at first. Each note, already chilling, rang throughout the spacious chamber, adding to the macabre feeling. Anna shivered, even though she was perfectly warm. The melody soon slowed and became melancholy. The tempo seemed to match that of water droplets slowly dripping off a rooftop after a large storm, adding a mere trickle to the flood that came before. The song transformed once more into a brighter emotion. Anna tried to pinpoint what it was. It wasn't quite happiness. She realized it was *hope*. The song was about hope.

When he finished, she spoke first. "It's beautiful. What is it about?

Chris continued to play an improvisational melody. "Addiction. It's an addict's tale. I was first inspired to write it when I studied the effects of drugs on people in school. It made me start my research into curing addictions."

"I thought you were still taking piano lessons?"

"I am. I'll never be too good to learn."

They didn't say much afterwards. He played music late into the night. Anna listened and watched the raindrops on the windows.

—-

Anna woke up bright and early the next day. She was still dazed from last night. She wasn't quite sure where their relationship was going, but she liked him for sure. She thought about his goodnight kiss last night and wondered if it was a dream. She could still feel the tingle of his warm lips on hers. She could still smell his pleasant scent as he leaned in and put his hand on the side of her face. Surely it wasn't a dream. The kiss was gentle and cautious—sweeter than she would have expected from him. She was smiling absentmindedly as she walked into the kitchen.

"I take it you had a nice time with Dr. Jamison?" Brittany inquired slyly.

Anna made a face. "Don't call him that. I always think of Chris's father instead."

Chris's board results had come in. As he suspected, he did not fail. However, he still had to wait a year before beginning an internship. Anna sat down. "I did have a wonderful time, though. I think I am beginning to like Chris," she blushed.

Brittany laughed. "You'd better get ready because Chris called and asked you to breakfast this morning. It seems he likes you too. "

"Oh, he called you?"

"Well, he tried getting a hold of you... but somebody never answers their phone," Brittany said pointedly as she walked out of the kitchen with her morning smoothie.

Anna dashed for her phone. Sure enough, she saw a couple of messages and a missed call from Chris. She smacked her forehead in exasperation. "Why is it so hard for me to remember this walkie talkie telephone?" she mumbled angrily.

Brittany chuckled and called from the living room. "It'll probably take you some time to get used to. Don't worry! Chris understands. He wasn't upset at all. We just made fun of you for about 10 minutes. "

"At least my struggles are entertaining to you two," Anna deadpanned.

"They are! I'll be thinking about them all day at work. I must get going now. You better get ready. He'll be here in 30 minutes." Brittany was quickly out the door and the ding of the elevator could be heard shortly after. Anna decided to wash up and put on her brand-new navy blue dress. She slipped on her sweater and shoes and almost immediately heard a knock at the door. She swung it open, already elated.

"You have good timing! I just put my shoes on and—"

Anna stopped as she stared into familiar brown eyes. *Chris doesn't have brown eyes,* she thought. Instead, a disheveled, exhausted-looking Elijah stood in the doorway.

Before she could react, he spoke. "Anna I need you to come with me." There was urgency in his voice.

"Elijah! What are you doing here? Is something wrong?"

Elijah spoke quickly, which was unusual for him. "Your father has had an accident. He's been admitted into Mercy Hospital St Louis. Your mother is there with him. The others had to stay home. Your mother asked me to come get you. She says she hears your father say your name at night. His spine is injured badly. They will operate on him soon. We have to hurry."

Anna stood there in shock. Elijah tugging on her hand snapped her back to reality. Unable to process everything, she grabbed her bag and followed Elijah outside. There was a taxi waiting for them.

"What happened, Eli?" she asked as they got in.

Elijah explained while the driver pulled onto the highway. "Our barn was damaged in a storm a few days ago. Some raccoons and coyotes have been trying to get in and attack the livestock. When we had to miss the market, your father came by with your brothers to help us with the repairs. I can't tell you what a godsend their help was. Halfway through, it started storming again. Harder this time. Your father was in the beams when the structure began to collapse. We tried to get to him in time, but the structure fell a few seconds later. Levi was crushed in between the beams. We had to get the lift to pull him out. He was still holding up when they drove him to see Dr. Kimberly, but she sent him to Mercy as his condition worsened. I went with your mother there. They figured it would be faster than mail if I went to get you. So, here I am."

Anna took this in quietly. She was known for being calm in emergencies. "Thank you for caring for my mother, Eli. My family needs our support right now. You were right to get me."

The remainder of the drive was silent until they pulled into an airport parking lot.

"We're flying?" Anna turned to Elijah with a start. It was highly uncommon in their order, but it was allowed during emergencies.

Elijah just grabbed Anna's hand. "Just stay near me. I'll keep you safe. I promise."

Anna nodded as a calm washed over her. She hadn't seen him in a while, but Elijah always meant what he said. She had faith that God had sent him to bring her back.

Elijah took care of checking in and was with her through the entire ordeal. His father had flown once before and had taught him the basics, in case he ever needed it. Anna had little time to process the procedure.

Everything was happening so suddenly; it felt like she wasn't part of reality anymore.

They soon boarded the plane and were on their way to St Louis. Elijah was still holding Anna's hand as they flew. She subconsciously rested her head on his shoulder and soon drifted off to sleep, still tired from last night. Despite the urgency of the situation, she felt at peace flying through the clouds with this man that she'd known since childhood.

As Elijah watched her fall asleep on his arm, he couldn't help but feel content. He leaned back and let the satisfaction and happiness wash over him. He hadn't felt this since Anna left. He hadn't mentioned it, but it was actually his idea to get Anna himself. Her mother had been too distraught to think about much. She had no idea how to reach Anna. After he convinced Abigail that he could bring her back, he was on the next flight to Chicago.

He watched her chest rise and fall as she breathed. *I have to tell her, but not yet,* he thought. She was already going through a lot. He didn't want to overwhelm her. He decided to just enjoy the moment. He looked at the woman he had loved for years. He knew he wanted to be with her anywhere she went. Hand in hand. *I love you, Anna.*

—-

Anna sat in the waiting room as the surgeons worked to save her father. He had been unconscious when they arrived, but she held his hand and spoke with him regardless. She was convinced he could hear her, and her thoughts were confirmed by squeezes from his hand. She had held it until the aides came to take him to his operation. She now looked at a text message from Chris on her phone. She had sent him a hurried message about the situation as they boarded the plane. She looked at his brief response.

Okay. I'll be there soon.

Be there soon? she wondered. *He's coming to St. Louis?* Sure enough, he showed up 30 minutes after she did. However, he didn't say much. He asked Anna some specifics about her father's condition. She didn't know, so he donned a lab coat and went to speak with the doctors. She could hear the whispers from the hospital staff. Apparently, he was somewhat famous among the medical community for graduating medical school in his teens. *Why couldn't he tell me more about my father? Why can't any of the doctors do that?* She looked over at Elijah, who was finally asleep after three days awake. *Without him, I wouldn't have known for several days.*

The sound of the operating room exit slamming open jolted him awake. Chris, in surgical attire, walked out with a clipboard in a hurried manner.

"Good news. There was a time when we thought he wasn't going to make it, but he somehow rallied and got through the woods. Your father is going to be okay."

He pulled off his mask. "They wouldn't let me touch him, of course. Not enough experience. After some convincing, they allowed me to observe. I've seen cases like this before. He's lucky to be alive. How much he'll recover remains to be seen."

Anna's eyes were wet with joy. Chris moved to sit next to her, but Elijah suddenly jumped up.

"So that's it? Mr. Miller will definitely be okay?"

"Yes. They're finishing up with him right now, but I wanted to come out and tell you." Chris said slowly, with Elijah already furiously pumping his hand in a firm handshake. He rubbed his thin fingers afterwards, wondering who this man was.

Elijah spoke with gratitude. "Thank you very much, doctor. We are forever in your debt."

"Of course. Who—"

Chris was cut off as Elijah moved in front of Anna. "Anna, now that we know your father will be okay, there's something I have to say.

It might not be the best time, but I can't wait any longer. I should have told you the day you were leaving, but I couldn't. I wanted to tell you on the plane, but you had too much on your mind. But I have to tell you now."

And, so he did. He told her that he had loved her for many years now. He talked about the adventures and laughter they had shared from since they were very little. He described the moment he knew he wanted to spend his life with her. He talked about the many times he almost told her his feelings.

"I wanted to tell you sooner. I should have told you sooner, but I was too worried about losing you. But since you've gone, I've felt this burning fire in my gut because you didn't know. It wasn't until then that I realized I had to tell you, regardless of your response."

Anna stood in shocked silence. She was already very emotional from the news about her father. She wondered what Elijah meant by "too much on her mind," as there was still quite a lot. He was usually a man of few words. She must have had these words in his mind for a long time.

He took her hand in his and held it. "And I mean that. I would never pressure you to do something you don't want. To *feel* a way you don't feel. I just wanted you to know, and tomorrow seemed too far away."

Anna stared at him unblinkingly. She felt paralyzed by the hurricane of emotions whirling through her. She wondered if Elijah knew this. She finally managed the strength to glance over at Chris. His face was unreadable, but he set down his clipboard, threw up his hands, and walked out.

"Elijah, I..." she managed.

He patted her hand. "You don't have to say anything right now. Think about it. Or don't. Don't feel obligated to do anything. No matter what happens, I'll love you. I'll love you as a life partner or as a friend, depending on what you need. Just take your time."

With those words, he let go of her hand, put on his hat, and strolled away as if nothing happened.

—-

The next two months were a complex time for Anna. She and her mother were overjoyed at her father's recovery, but he was still bedridden for the foreseeable future. In addition, the steep hospital bills suddenly left the family in debt with the primary breadwinner unable to work. Anna responded to this by taking on a second job at a nearby diner. Days passed by in a blur, but not the kind that comes with fun times. For Anna, this was the blur of sleep deprivation and exhaustion. After a long day at the Jamison clinic, she threw herself into washing dishes and sweeping floors. She often didn't come home until well after midnight, sometimes catching a worried look from Brittany before collapsing on her bed. After a few short hours of sleep, her day would begin again.

Brittany had insisted upon helping with the family bills. Her initial financial support was how the family avoided bankruptcy. However, much of her assets were tied up in physical investments and stocks, and couldn't be quickly liquified. Still, Anna couldn't thank her enough and promised she would repay her. She had already used her previously untouched credit card to make her way back to Chicago.

Anna knew the grind of hard times and took it in stride, but she worried her body couldn't hold on much longer. Every night, she prayed that she wouldn't become seriously ill. She needed to be healthy to work for her family. However, she could feel herself breaking down. She had already developed a foreboding cough that wouldn't go away.

Of course, there was also what happened in the waiting room. In her rare moments of free time, she worked on a letter she was writing to Elijah. They had a lot to discuss. She had written many versions, but most of them ended up in the trash. She just couldn't find a good way to say what she felt.

She also needed to talk to Chris. He had effectively disappeared. Anna tried to make time to see him, but their schedules never seemed to be compatible. The few times she had seen him were at the office, and he always left in a hurry. Working in what seemed like despair and hopelessness, she really wished he were there to offer reassurance. Brittany had angrily called him a "fair-weather lover."

When Anna suggested he simply didn't have time, Brittany waved it off. "No, Anna. That's the oldest, flimsiest excuse boys will give you. The truth is that they will make time if they want to give you time."

This only served to further depress Anna.

—-

Anna got out of the car and waved goodbye to Kelly, who had dropped her off. Autumn seemed to come early in this city. Although it was still warm during the day, she could already see golden brown leaves skating across the sidewalks as the wind blew them through the city. The cool wind exacerbated her cough, so she walked quickly towards the condominium's front door. She only had an hour to shower and change before her shift at the diner. As she walked through the glass doors into the lobby, she saw a familiar face. Chris stood by the back wall, near the mailboxes.

He took a few steps towards her. "Anna, we need to talk."

"Hm. No. You're probably busy. I wouldn't want to keep you." She turned to walk towards the elevators.

He blocked her path and she tried to go around him. He moved again. This continued for a few moments. "Anna, I'm leaving," he finally said.

She stopped. "What?"

"To Singapore. Next week."

When Anna didn't respond, he continued "I found a clinic there that would let me work before I turn eighteen. They like the research I've done about addiction treatments and want to be a part of it."

"Good for you. Is that all you came here to do? To boast?" She headed towards the elevators again.

"Well, no. I actually came to give you this." She stopped and turned around. He took a thin envelope out of his peacoat and handed it to her.

"What is this?" she asked, as she opened it. It was a check for the remainder of her hospital debt.

"It's from Brittany too," he said hurriedly as she tried to angrily shove it back into his hands.

"What?"

"Well, actually it's from the bank. We had to work together to get a loan. It's in our name, so you can pay her back over time. This way, you don't have to work yourself to death."

Anna looked at him. "Brittany says you're a fair-weather lover."

Chris smiled thinly. "I know. She called to chew me out multiple times. She really cares for you."

Anna took out the check and stared at it. "Why did someone like you need to get a loan anyway?"

He looked away. "Well, the truth is..." He paused to chuckle. "The truth is I'm kind of broke at the moment. My family really didn't approve of my move to Singapore and have threatened to cut me off. They want me here to run their businesses. My father was the only one that supported my decision. It was only because of him and your cousin that we were able to get a loan at all."

Anna felt some pity for him. "That's too bad. I had no idea."

He waved it off. "Don't feel bad. I suspected this would happen and did it anyway. I just came here to drop off the cashier's check with Brittany, but she said I should give it to you personally because I owe you an apology. I really am sorry, Anna. I genuinely have been busy preparing for Singapore, but I should have been there for you."

Anna looked down at her shoes. "I'm sorry you had to hear what Elijah said. He didn't know who you were." She looked up at him and took a breath. "About that..."

He closed the gap between them and grabbed her gently by the shoulders. "You don't have to explain it. A few moments after that Amish boy spontaneously confessed his love to you, I knew how you felt. I've seen how you look at me, and I've seen how you look at him. There's no comparison."

He looked away as he continued. "I will confess that I was a little disappointed at first, but I recognized the passion and fever in his voice as he talked about you. He had hope for a life with you. Everyone needs hope."

Anna didn't say anything, but her smile told Chris everything he needed. He took a step back and returned it. "Of course, I won't forget our time together. I'll always be here if you need a friend. That is, if you want to stay in touch?"

Anna's smile widened. "Yes, I would."

—-

It was surprising to Anna how quickly life could change. With her family's financial troubles temporarily relieved, Anna didn't need to work her second job. This allowed her body to finally get enough rest again, and her cough began to clear. She still worked hard, of course. She created a payment plan for repaying Brittany and followed it. Additionally, she had received news that her father was walking again and was expected to make a full recovery. Anna felt as if the sun had risen in her life after a long, cold night.

She also had time to finalize a letter to Elijah. She sat down and wrote from her heart. After she was done, she read what she had written:

Dearest Elijah,

I was delighted to hear the news about Dad's progress. Please continue to watch over him. I know he'll be itching to get back to work, but he must take it easy.

I am sorry it has taken me so long to write to you. I could blame it on being busy, but truthfully... I guess I just wasn't sure how to say how I felt. I've had that problem with you since we were kids, and I guess you know how I feel. Sometimes we're still looking for the words to say...

Why didn't you tell me sooner, Eli? Of course I feel the same way. I never dared hope that you shared my thoughts. I suppose I feared that if I told you first, that hope might be gone. I know now that hope is never truly gone. It stays with us, and if we dare to embrace it, it shines a light on the path God meant for us to walk.

I must say that we will need to work on your conversational timing, though. What a moment you chose to say those things!

I'll need to stay in the city a while longer to work, but after that I am coming home. I'm coming home, Elijah. I have loved Chicago and I love Brittany, but this experience has only helped me realize where I need to be. I look forward to seeing you again.

Forever yours,

Anna.

She smiled and folded the letter into an envelope. As she walked down to the mailroom, she thought about her mother, father, and siblings. She thought about living a life with Elijah and raising a family of their own. She laughed as she thought about what her friends would say about that. There was no doubt in her mind that was her home. She would be there soon.

THE AMISH HEART

ABBY BARKER

"I'll only be gone for a little while, Ma. It's a seasonal position so it's only for the summer. I'll be home before you know it."

"Soon isn't soon enough, Annie. I want you here with Pa and I working around the house, not in some zoo."

"Nancy pulled all sorts of strings to get me this job. You told me I could go on rumspringa. Why are you trying to take it back?"

Annie's mother looked at her with defeated eyes but didn't say a word. She knew how much planning and excitement her daughter put into this getaway. There would be no way to convince her hardheaded girl to revise her plan now. She let out a deep sigh and handed back the tote bag she had been clinging to as an attempt to force Annie to stay.

"Thanks, Ma. This will be good for me, and you. Nancy's going to be here any minute now and I really do need to finish packing."

Annie kissed her mother on the cheek and went back to meticulously choosing which of her old-fashioned Amish outfits could pass as casual English fashion. It wasn't easy. Other than a handful of pajama sets that she convinced her mother to let her buy – only for wearing around the house – she mostly had long skirts and shawls. She'd have to go shopping with Nancy when they got to the city.

Annie felt a wave of excitement and nerves wash over her. Not only was she starting a job working with animals, her one true passion, but she'd be doing it in Chicago. She thought back on the times when she and Nancy were kids and they talked about getting an apartment together somewhere exciting. It wasn't until she met Nancy that she learned anything about English life at all.

Nancy's family is English, but living so close to their town her parents were longtime family friends of Annie's neighbors. The Millers didn't have any children of their own, so when Nancy came to visit they'd send her over to Annie's to play. Even coming from two different worlds, the two girls had plenty in common. They liked climbing trees, playing hide and seek in the field, and most of all playing veterinarian. They would wander around the farm diagnosing the animals with any number of made-up illnesses and curing them with equally fictional remedies. The goats were easily susceptible to Pink-horn-itis, which was easily cured by a health dose of fairy dust, while the horses could often be found suffering from the Tap Dancing Flu. That illness had to run its course, but singing an upbeat song and dancing along could expedite the healing process.

The only difference between them was when they were old enough to go to college Nancy was the only one who went. Annie's parents instead she stay at home and learn how to take care of the farm. While Nancy worked towards her veterinary degree, Annie cooked, cleaned, and tended to the livestock. Annie understood why her parents didn't let her go to school, but that didn't mean she was happy about it. So when Nancy heard of an open assistant zookeeper position at the city zoo where she was interning she jumped at the chance for Annie to apply. The job only lasted a couple months, filling in when needed during the zoo's busy summer season, which made it a perfect fit for Annie. She'd have to go back to her town eventually or risk getting shunned by her entire community, including her parents.

Nancy eventually convinced her bosses that Annie would be a good fit for the job, what with her experience working with farm animals and above all else, her passion. They agreed she would come stay with Nancy in the city while she worked. Their childhood dreams were finally coming true, even if it was temporary. Annie's daydreaming was interrupted by a honk from outside. She shoved whatever item of clothing she had in her hand into her bag and bolted out the door. Nancy jumped out of the driver's seat and ran to meet her friend. The two girls jumped up and down squealing, both equally excited to finally live together.

"Annie, Annie, Annie, Ann! Get your ass in the car!"

Nancy clasped her hand over her mouth and looked around nervously hoping Annie's parents weren't within earshot. Luckily, they weren't as quick to great her as Annie was.

"Whoops. I'll try and keep the swearing to a minimum until we're on the road."

"Well let's get on the damn road already!"

The girls fell into a fit of laughter just as Annie's parents joined them on the lawn.

"What could you two possibly be laughing about already?"

"Nothing, Ma. We're just excited is all," Annie said, stifling a giggle. Her mother had calmed down considerably since their conversation earlier, but jokes involving swear words would only upset her again. She uncrossed her arms to give her daughter a hug.

"Be good and be careful, sweetheart. Zoo animals are not like farm animals, and English people are not like Amish people. No offence, Nancy, I just want you to be prepared for city life."

"Ma, I think you're being a little dramatic. It's not like the English are a completely different species."

Annie mother just pursed her lips and stayed silent. She didn't want to argue with her daughter right before she left for the summer.

"I'll be fine. Nancy will be there."

"That's what I'm afraid off," she teased playfully.

After a final round of hugs for her parents, and a gentle scolding from Annie's mother to Nancy about not corrupting her little girl, the pair set out for Chicago. They only made it about two blocks before erupting into laughter again. It had been a few months since they'd seen each other last and they were overflowing with pent up energy. Annie had her friends in town, but they were often more reserved and frankly more boring than Nancy. She enjoyed Amish life just as much as the next girl, but sometimes she needed an outlet.

"Annie-bananie, you are going to crap your pants when you see the city. The only horses and buggies you're going to see will be shuttling tourists between steakhouses and the Sears Tower."

"I don't really have a lot of clothes so I'm going to have to be careful about how much crapping I'm doing in them."

"I'll take you downtown and get you plenty of new outfits to crap in. Don't you worry."

The city was a few hours drive from Annie's town but it felt like no time at all. The two girls chatted away nonstop for the entire trip. Nancy went through her entire mental list of favorite restaurants, shops, and museums in between Annie's lamenting about how stifling her parents have been ever since she decided to spend the summer in Chicago. While they respected her decision, they didn't like it. They spent the last few weeks doing everything they could to convince her to stay and giving her the cold shoulder when she wouldn't change her mind. She felt guilty at times, but knew this was the right choice for her.

When the skyline finally came into view Annie gasped. The staggered peaks of the downtown buildings formed a giant fence standing between where she was now and where she wanted to be. The sight overwhelmed her. She'd never seen anything so incredibly massive in her entire life. The biggest building in her town was a two-story barn. She hoped the giant fence she pictured also had a gate.

Nancy drove into the city, the streets slowly narrowing, until she came to a modest apartment building next to a wide, green park. Just on the other side of the park was a seemingly never-ending lake.

"We're home!" Nancy yelled, pulling into a parking space next to the building. "Wait until you see the view from our living room. You can almost see Michigan across the lake!"

Annie was still reeling from all the new things she saw in this state, she didn't know if she'd be able to handle another whole state.

***

After excitedly riding an elevator for the first time, flipping through every channel on TV, and marveling at Nancy's expansive and colorful wardrobe Annie worked up an appetite. There wasn't always a huge variety when it came to meals back home. The food was always good

– fresh vegetables, milk from their cow, bread straight from the oven – but supper could get a bit repetitive over time. She knew Chicago to be filled with every type of cuisine imaginable, but there was one thing she'd been dying to try ever since she decided to move in with Nancy.

"Nance, we have to get deep dish pizza, like, right now. If I don't have a slice of famous Chicago deep dish in front of me soon I'll totally lose it."

"Okay, okay chill out. We'll get you that cheesy, delicious slice. We gotta go to Lou Malnati's. It's the absolute best."

"Yes, that's all I want. Maybe I should change first before we go."

Annie realized that she was still wearing her long, black skirt and button-up blouse from back home. The conservative outfit didn't seem to her to be the most fashionable option but she didn't have much else to choose from. Luckily, Nancy was there to reassure her.

"No way. You look rad and a little bit vintage-y in that getup. People are gonna think you're some kind of fashion icon."

She linked her arm through Annie's and pulled her towards the door. A true Chicagoan, Nancy had no time to waste when it came to deep dish. The girls walked through the bustling city talking and laughing, the excitement from the day's events not quite worn off. Annie was fascinated by how much life there was in streets. Shops and restaurants had their doors open, families walked together through the park, and friends just like them made their ways to get their own delicious dinners. The contrast to her little town was striking. She only saw groups of people this large when she went to the market or church, but just walking through the streets she encountered the odd farmer or woman also on their way into town, but nothing so lively as this and never at night. She couldn't help but smile at the various people she passed, and to her surprise, they more often than not smiled back. She couldn't wait to tell her mother how wrong she was about people in the city not being friendly.

At the restaurant they were seated right away, despite it being fairly crowded. Annie didn't even have to look at the menu. She excitedly told the waiter exactly what she wanted the moment they sat down. While they waited for their food she noticed a young man across the restaurant looking over at her. He had dark, curly hair and eyes to match. Every time she caught him glancing over he'd smile a little before returning to his meal. Eventually Annie couldn't take it anymore. She had to know why he was doing this.

"Nancy, do you see that guy over there? He keeps staring at me and smiling. It's super weird."

"He probably thinks you're cute! You should go over and talk to him."

"No way! That would be even weirder."

"No it wouldn't. He keeps looking at you. He obviously wants to talk to you. At the very least you can ask him what his deal is."

Annie glanced over toward the man and noticed he was staring at her once again. That was the last straw. She stood up from the table and marched over to him.

"Excuse me, I couldn't help but notice that you couldn't help but notice me. Can I ask why you keep staring at me?"

"I'm sorry! I didn't mean to freak you out. I just saw your clothing and thought you might be Amish. I'm Amish too, or at least I was, or maybe I might be again. I still haven't decided yet, but it's nice to see a familiar face or skirt, I mean."

Annie's face flushed. She didn't expect him to be so friendly and felt a little embarrassed for approaching him so hostilely.

"I should have just come up to talk to you instead of making you storm over like that. It's not the best first impression, I know. My name's Sean. What are you doing so far from home?"

"I'm staying with a friend of mine," she gestured behind her toward Nancy. "I start working at the zoo tomorrow."

"The zoo! That's definitely not what I was expecting but I'd love to hear more. Would you want to meet up for coffee sometime, when you're not busy tending to the animals of course?"

Annie walked over to this man expecting to tell him off, but instead he's asked her on a date? Chicago was exceeding her expectations. She felt a little guilty dating outside of her community, but Sean said he was Amish, or used to be at least. That was close enough, right? She decided what her parents didn't know wouldn't hurt them.

"I'm sure I'll have some free time while they sleep. Coffee sounds lovely."

"Great! Give me your phone number and I'll call you sometime."

"That might be a problem. I don't actually have a phone yet, but I can give you my friend's number and you can reach me there."

"Ah, you're fresh from Amish land then," Sean teased. "Her number will work just fine."

Annie recited the digits off to him before saying a polite goodbye and returning to her table. When she got there Nancy practically crawled over the table to get the details of their interaction.

"Who is that guy? You were over there for a long time. Why was he staring at you? Was I right? Does he think you're cute? Do you think he's cute?"

Annie relayed the conversation in acute detail, still excited about the prospect of her first big city date. Nancy nodded along happily, interjecting occasionally.

"No way! What are the frickin' chances that on your first night here you'd run into another Amish person, or formally Amish or whatever. I mean, of course he asked you on a date, too, you're frickin' amazing. Am I saying frickin' a lot again? I'm just so frickin' excited for you!"

Annie laughed. Nancy was almost more enthusiastic about this than she was.

"He's cute, right? Most of the guys I'm used to seeing are dressed for church."

"Oh yeah, he's definitely cute, like, super cute. You done good, my friend."

When Annie crawled into bed that night she had to force herself to sleep. She couldn't help but repeat the conversation with Sean over and over again in her head. It wasn't much, but it consumed her thoughts. As she drifted off she couldn't tell if the butterflies in her stomach were mostly because she'd start her new job in the morning, or if they were from him.

She was awoken the next morning by Nancy tickling her feet at the end of the bed.

"Get up Annie! The animals wait for no man, or woman."

Annie groaned and giggled before rolling out of bed and slowly getting dressed. Nancy had made coffee and was waiting for her in the kitchen.

"Either chug a cup of hot coffee our grab a to-go mug out of the cabinet and take it with you. Don't want to be late on your first day, or my one hundredth."

"Is it really your one hundredth day of work?"

"Man, you really do need some coffee. I'm only joking with you, but seriously let's go. It's only a twenty minute walk from here."

Annie filled a thermos with coffee and the two girls flew out the door. She was glad to have the brisk walk to wrangle in her nerves. This was going to be her first official job that also happened to be her dream. With the tons of excitement she felt also came a lot of pressure. Most of all, if she screwed up then she'd have to face her mother's "I told you so." It turned out she had nothing to worry about however because when they finally made it through the entrance of the zoo they were greeted by the most warm and welcoming zookeeper. Kyra was a pleasantly plump blonde woman with as much passion for animals as for hospitality. She began her introduction as Nancy politely excused herself – with a wink and reassuring shoulder pat to Annie – from the conversation as she was needed elsewhere.

"Annie! We're so happy to have you here. Nancy talked endlessly about you and your love for animals, we absolutely couldn't pass up the chance to invite you. My name's Kyra and I'm going to show you around today. I run HR here at the zoo so as long as you're doing your job and doing it well you unfortunately won't have to see me much after today! Let's get you your uniform and then I'll introduce you to some of our residents and your supervisor. You two will have plenty to talk about. He's Amish too! You'll be working mostly with the big cats, but I'll show you everything!"

Kyra slipped that fact seamlessly into her on boarding speech but Annie caught it immediately. Her new boss was Amish, or used to be. Is this Nancy got her the job? Also, what were the chances that she'd meet two Amish men within days of getting to the city? Was she some sort of magnet for people like her?

After changing into her new uniform, Annie followed Kyra around the zoo as she breathlessly explained the inner workings of the place as well as each of the animals' personalities in detail.

"Daphne and Dylan are our river otters and they spend most of their day playing tag in the pool and hamming it up for the guests. Those two a real attention seekers, let me tell you. They'll swim back and forth against the glass just trying to get someone to look at them."

Eventually they made it to the bear enclosure. Two brown bears slept cozily under a tree together, shaded by the branches above. They made soft noises in their sleep but were otherwise completely still.

"Now these two don't look like much right now but when they're awake boy are they trouble. They're not bad bears by any means, just mischievous. Don't turn your back on them for one second, even through the fence. They want whatever you have and will snack food right out of your hands. They're not trying to hurt you but they're bears. They can't help it. Oh, and their names are Ben and Jerry. We rescued them from a man who really liked ice cream and owning animals that shouldn't be kept as pets."

Annie watched their furry backs move up and down as the breathed. Even from outside the enclosure the bears were impressive. She couldn't wait to see them in action. She wondered when that might be.

"When do I start with my actual duties?"

"Well, we have a few more animals and a handful of people left to introduce you to today, but I'll drop you off with Andrew in a bit. He's a little shy, but a good boss. I think he prefers to spend his time with the cats rather than other people, but he's a real sweetheart. He'll show you the ropes!"

Annie followed Kyra around the zoo for a little while longer, meeting different keepers and animals along the way, before making it to the big cathouse. Once inside, Kyra lead them to a basement room set up like a restaurant kitchen. A surprisingly tall, blonde man stood at a silver counter hacking away at a hunk of meat. He didn't appear to notice them walk in, or he at least didn't acknowledge them.

"Andrew, this is your new assistant zookeeper, Annie. I want you to show her all it is you do around here."

Now that he had been directly addressed, Andrew looked away from his task and flashed the two women a bright smile.

"Nice to meet you, Annie. Want to chop up some raw meat with me?"

Kyra smiled and said, "That's the spirit!" before leaving Annie and Andrew alone in the prep kitchen. Andrew wordlessly gestured at the sink, seeming to indicate Annie should wash her hands before joining in. She rushed over to it, eager to make a good impression but nervous about being alone in a room with a man. The only men she was permitted to be alone with back home were family members, and even then only the close ones like her father and grandfather. She knew it wasn't a big deal in an English work place, but she couldn't help but feel a faint blush wash over her cheeks when she joined Andrew at the counter. It didn't help that she found his sandy hair and quiet eyes very attractive.

"So what you want to do is grab a hunk of meat, like this, and cut it into pieces, like this. Please don't be intimidated by skill level. I've been doing this for quite some time now."

He was clearly teasing her, and even though she understood this she still took extra care when cutting up her first piece. His gentle humor relaxed her nerves a bit and she felt comfortable enough to tease him right back.

"Is this right? Should I hold the knife by the blade?"

"Oh, yes. Everyone knows the handle is the best part of the knife for cutting meat. Just make sure to grip the blade extremely tight so that you don't lose control of it."

"Okay, perfect, I think I've got it. You're an excellent teacher."

"That's why they keep me around!"

They both laughed at that but then fell silent for a few moments as they continued their task. They were both comfortable with the silence but curious about each other. It didn't take long for Andrew to speak up.

"So, I hope you don't mind me asking this, but Nancy says you're Amish, right? What brings you to a zoo in Chicago?"

"I was about to ask you the same thing!" When Andrew looked surprised she clarified. "Kyra told me that 'we have a lot in common.'" They both laughed. "Nancy and I have been friends forever, but when she got the chance to go to school and get a veterinary degree I had to stay home and basically get a degree in housekeeping. When Nancy said she could get me this job I jumped at the chance to get out of there for a while before I have to marry a nice Amish boy and settle down."

"Another probing question, why do you want to go back? It doesn't sound like you want that kind of life, I know I didn't."

Annie thought about this for a moment. In a way, Andrew was right. An old-fashioned Amish marriage didn't really appeal to her, but she also couldn't imagine her life as anything other than Amish. There had to be a middle ground somewhere but she had no idea where that might be. Where did he find his middle ground? She could only reply, "I don't know. I guess we'll have to wait and see. Why did you decide to give it all up?"

"I raised cows on my family's farm. Just cows. Do you know how boring cows are? I wanted to do more than breed cattle and I couldn't believe that God would hate me for following my dreams, you know? My parents weren't happy, but I was."

They had finished the meat chopping and had now moved to putting it all into buckets to bring out to the big cats. Annie mentioned liking lions and Andrew agreed, but told her that the jaguar was his favorite.

"She's the queen of the big cat house. She's not as physically active as some of the other cats but when you look into her eyes as she's sitting up on her perch you can tell that she's looking back. She really sees you."

Annie felt an inadvertent smile spread across her face as she listened to the warmth and awe in Andrew's voice as he talked about the big cat. He truly cared for and admired the animals that he worked with. She found herself wondering if those feelings extended to any other parts of his life. Annie blushed when she realized where her mind had wandered. She wasn't even sure if Andrew was interested in her in that way, but part of her hoped he was. Finding romance wasn't her intention when she decided to come to Chicago but first with Sean and now Andrew she didn't know what to think.

Her mind raced as she and Andrew carried the heavy bucket of meat together to feed the big cats. Going from no romance in her life whatsoever to two potential crushes in 24 hours was overwhelming. She didn't know if she could handle one, let alone both men on her mind. She had almost convinced herself to give up on the idea of Andrew and focus on the guy who already showed an interest in her when Andrew's hand slipped on the bucket handle and brushed up against hers. Sparks like electric shocks shot up through her arm. That simple touch almost made her drop the bucket on the floor. She couldn't look at him directly but out of the corner of her eye she could see a small smile on his lips and a flush on his cheeks. He wasn't moving his hand. So much for forgetting about Andrew.

The walk to the enclosures felt like it lasted for miles when it was just down the hall. When the pair finally made it to the jaguar's cage and set down the bucket Annie felt like she could finally breath again. She didn't know what it was about him that made her feel so lightheaded but she was doing her best to control it. Andrew unlocked the door to the first part of the cage were they'd be able to toss the meat into the enclosure through the bars. It wasn't the most traditionally romantic spot, but the space was small and they had to stand shoulder to shoulder in order for them both to fit. The jaguar knew it was feeding time and began pacing back and forth along the bars. Seeing the predator up close sent a shiver down Annie's spine. The cat had all the majesty and intelligence Andrew described.

"Annie, meet Camilla. I like to think she gets excited to see me but I know it's really just the food. Want to toss her some meat?"

Annie nodded and stuck her hand in the bucket. The meat was cold and slimy but it didn't bother her. She grabbed a hunk and lobbed it through the bars and into the center of the enclosure. Camilla lunged for it and gobbled it up in one bite.

"She's fast!"

"If these bars weren't here she wouldn't hesitate to come after either of us and our bucket. We wouldn't get so far as the end of the hallway we came down before she pounced on us."

Annie looked startled.

"I'm only teasing! There's no way she's getting out of her enclosure."

When she didn't look convinced Andrew placed both hands on her shoulders for reassurance. Another shot of electricity ran through her entire body. He stared right into her eyes and she was frozen like a deer in headlights. He inched closer to her without removing his hands or breaking eye contact. She didn't move away. Before she could realize what was happening, Andrew pushed her up against the bars of Camilla's cage and kissed her passionately on the mouth. She felt Camilla brush past the backs of her legs from the other side of the bars. It was dangerous to be this close – to both the animal and this boy – but she kissed him back anyways. When he finally pulled away he looked sheepish.

"Whoops. I don't know what came over me. Some sort of animal instinct, I guess," they both laughed breathlessly. "Not exactly what you were expecting on your first day of work, huh?"

She touched her lips softly and chuckled. It was her first kiss.

"No. Not exactly."

Annie was shell-shocked. On the one hand, she never imagined a kiss would feel that way. Her parents and other adults in her community barely ever showed or talked about physical affection, which led her to believe it must not be that great. She was wrong. But on the other hand, she now had to think about Sean. She wasn't the type to see two men at once and now she had to make a choice.

Andrew, now embarrassed by his actions, took Annie's clipped response to mean wasn't interested. She thought it would be best to let him think this while she figured out what she wanted to do. It wouldn't be fair to lead him on if she really ended up liking Sean. Plus, she couldn't forget the expiration date on her time in Chicago. She'd have to go home in three months. Probably.

After feeding time, Kyra came back to collect Annie. There were a few more logistics and some paperwork they had to do before the end of the day. Andrew said an awkward "It was nice to meet you," to which Annie responded with a small smile and a wave. She hoped he didn't feel too embarrassed about the kiss. She wished she could tell him how much she enjoyed it without jumping the gun. She'd been in the city for less than 48 hours and things had already gotten complicated. For the first time since she arrived she felt a pang of longing for the simplicity of home.

A week went by before she heard from Sean. Andrew started to relax around her again. They'd joke around while preparing meals for all the big cats, tossing little chunks of raw meat at each other from across the room. It was flirtatious, but friendly – a speed Annie was comfortable with when it came to romance. She had all but given up on Sean and had even made plans with Andrew to hang out after work the next day when the boy from the pizza place called.

"ANNIE! Annie, Annie, Annie. You have a phone call. A good one!"

Nancy came barreling into Annie's room, cell phone raised above her head like an Olympic torch.

"Who is it?" Annie whispered, afraid the person on the other line could hear her friend's yelling.

"Oh, don't worry. I muted it. I think," she looked at the screen to double check. "Yep. Muted. It's that guy from Lou Malnati's! Sean, I think. He wants to talk to you! He wants to do *more* than talk to you."

Nancy winked, tossed the phone into Annie's hands, and waited in the doorway.

"Get out, loser! I'll tell you all about it afterwards. Don't sit there staring at me!"

After Nancy closed the door Annie took a deep breathe and unmated the phone.

"Hello?"

"Hey! Is this Annie?"

"Yes, it's me."

"Oh good. For a second I forgot you gave me your friend's number and thought it was a fake. I'm glad I was wrong. How are you?"

"I'm good. Just relaxing after a long day of chopping up animals to feed to other animals. I told you I work at a zoo, right? I'm not just a crazy person talking about chopping up animals."

She heard a laugh on the other line.

"You told me. Don't worry. Want to take a break from all that chopping and get dinner with me tomorrow?"

"Sure! As long as it's not raw meat."

Sean laughed again.

"Noted. I'll pick a place and text Nancy the details. See you tomorrow!"

It wasn't until after she hung up that she realized she'd already made plans with Andrew the next day. She had been so excited about Sean's call that she completely forgot. She should call Sean back and tell him her mistake, but did she want to?

"Nancy!"

Nancy appeared at Annie's bedroom door in less than a second. She'd been waiting outside.

"How did it go? Are you married now? Are you going to move away to a secluded island together?"

"What? No. Nancy, I have a little problem."

"What?"

"I might have accidentally agreed to hang out with Sean and Andrew at the same time."

"Oh boy, looks like you're gonna have to choose one. Who's it gonna be?"

"I don't know, Nancy! Sean was so nice at the restaurant, and so not my boss. But I can't forget that kiss. I mean, who knows if Andrew's even interested in me anymore though. Flinging hunks of raw meat at my head isn't exactly romantic."

"Well, duh, of course it is. Guys don't know how to deal with their feelings so they throw stuff at you and hope you figure it out."

"Ugh. What should I do?"

"Who do you like best?"

"I don't even know if I can like anyone at all! I have to go back home and marry a nice Amish boy like my mother wants anyways, not a formerly nice Amish boy. Why should I even bother?"

"Because it's fun! Plus, do you *have* to go back. I mean, I know it's been your plan and all but is that what you really want?"

"I don't know."

Annie slumped back onto her bed and closed her eyes. It's true, she couldn't imagine a life other than an Amish one but that didn't mean it wasn't possible. There would be plenty of consequences she'd have to face, but plenty of benefits too. She knew, though, that this was too big a choice to make based on a silly crush. She wouldn't give up being Amish for a boy, it would be for her.

Annie decided the next morning that she was going to try and hang out with both of them. She'd grab a coffee or something with Andrew after work and get out of there in time to meet Sean for dinner. She'd have to make a decision after that; Sean, Andrew, or neither.

After their shifts, Andrew took Annie to his favorite coffee shop nearby. The staff greeted him by name. He stopped in every morning before work to grab a cup. They ordered and found a table by the window.

"I'm glad we're finally getting to hang out, you know, not covered in meat," Andrew said with a teasing smile on his face.

"Oh, I'm still covered in meat. Washing my hands after work can only do so much."

"Well, it suits you then. I think you're cute, meat and all."

Annie blushed and took a sip of her coffee. So he was still interested. That made things more difficult. They talked about easy things – work, how another keeper almost let the chimps out of their enclosure, favorite foods – until Andrew asked when she was going home.

"Um, well, my job ends in two months so I'm only supposed to stay until the end of the summer."

Andrew swirled the dregs of his coffee around in his cup for a moment before responding.

"You should stay."

Annie felt more surprised by this than the kiss."

"Seriously. I could hire you fulltime. I like...working with you. You're a natural with the cats. Don't go back. Stay."

The sincerity in his eyes was overwhelming. It had only been a week but she had developed a strong connection with Andrew. They spent nearly every day together, just them and the cats. She knew she liked being around him, but she didn't realize how much until now. He reached out over the table and grabbed her rand, running his thumb softly over her palm. The electricity was back.

"You should stay."

She would stay. The decision she fretted over was made simple in that moment, even simpler than what she longed for back home. She'd stay in that coffee shop with him that evening – she didn't need to see Sean anymore – and she'd stay in the city with him chopping up bits of meat and tossing them to the big cats. She couldn't promise forever, it was too soon for that anyways, but she could promise now. Camilla might be the queen of the zoo, but Andrew made her feel like the queen of everything else.